BATHHOUSE STORIES

by

Robert Rahula

© 2016 Robert Rahula

robertrahula.com

facebook.com/robert.rahula

ALSO BY ROBERT RAHULA

NOVELS:

Messieurs
Panamaniac
Island of Misfits
Day Another Paradise In
One Last Fling
Bathhouse Stories
Conversation in a Belgian Bar
All the Yage in Reno
Exigent Circumstances

SHORT STORIES:

Horror Stories for Children

POETRY:

Trigger Points
Dentro Del Corazón Bloqueada
Camino
Migration
I Sing the Body Politic
Wonderland
From Whose Bourn
Poemas Españoles
Expat Poems

ANTHOLOGIES:

Half Life
The Essential Dan Landes

First Printing, 2018
ISBN 978-0-9994736-2-7

Alma-gator Press

Barcelona • Madrid • La Chorrera

"The road of excess leads to the palace of wisdom."
–William Blake

"But first it leads to more excess."
– Robert Rahula

Table of Contents

Chapter 1:   CIEGA SORDOMUDA

Ricardo was sitting in his favorite spot in the steam room of the bathhouse when he first saw the man walk in, or rather, when he first saw the man *feel* his way in. It always took a few minutes for anyone's eyes to adjust to the dim light in the steam room, so it was not unusual to see men hug the wall and move slowly when they first entered the dark steam room from the well-lit shower area located right outside the steam room doors. And so it was with this man. Ricardo watched him move slowly along the wall, as he eased into the steam room, the fingertips of his left hand gliding lightly along the wet wall, his right hand held up in front, chest-high, about a foot in front of him, in case he should encounter another naked body in the semi-darkness.

But you know, my friends, that's the whole point of a steam room—to ease your way blindly into the steamy heat; naked, of course, as are all the other men in the steam room. You drape your towel over your shoulder, and as you move around, first into the large main room with concrete steps set against the wall like an amphitheatre where some men sit, you will inevitably encounter, by touch, another man easing his way in the opposite direction. You both stop of course, to avoid colliding, and then hands gently feel each other, like ants greeting one another on the wall; first you gently feel his shoulder, to determine what way he is facing, then maybe gently down his front, to determine his size, how hairy he might be, whether he is slim or heavy, and then, if neither pulls away, you will feel further down, gently touching or taking hold of his cock, feeling it, gently moving your hand back and forth, as the other man, hopefully, is doing the same to you. And it does not matter, initially at least, whether the other man is well-endowed or not. The greeting in the darkened steam room is always the same, although it's true that if the other has a large cock or an erect cock or even if his cock just feels right to you, you will stay there longer, maybe start to rub the man's chest or his back with your other hand, and things may progress from there. And even if the man has a small cock, you still might linger a bit, masturbating him more as you stand there, because you never know, some cocks are deceptively small when limp, but grow nicely when aroused. But normally, after a few minutes of this ritual greeting, one of you will give the other a gentle tap goodbye on the shoulder, and you both will move on, further into the darkness, to greet other men, hopefully many more men, in the same silent anonymously intimate fashion.

And when I say that Ricardo was sitting in his favorite spot, I mean that he liked to sit on any of the concrete steps near the steam room door. There the dim light was the strongest, and from that position he could see each man who entered the steam room, especially the new men who had just arrived at the bathhouse: who had just paid their admission fee; who had just gotten undressed in the locker room; who had just walked to the showers and soaped themselves up, especially their most private parts, to prepare their bodies for other men; and who had just entered the steam room where their eyes had not yet adjusted to the dim light, so they instinctively raised a left arm to the wall for stability and direction, and moved blindly inward through the chamber that opened up to the large amphitheatre room where men came to relax after cruising through the pitch-black corridors that led away from the steam room. From that position Ricardo could stare at each new arrival, whose eyes could not yet stare back, and Ricardo could watch them move, could see their cocks, and he could assess his attraction to each, and decide whether he wished to stand up and be the first to approach them. On slow days in the bathhouse, when there were not many men, this position was quite useful, because attractive newcomers would not be available for long before one of the other men in the steam room might take them by the hand, whisper something in their ear, and lead them off to a room where, behind closed doors, they might engage in various acts of love—well, let's be honest—various acts of sex, some acts perhaps so intimate that one might be reluctant to describe them, but from which room the newcomer would eventually emerge, spent, exhausted, lips, cock, or ass perhaps a bit chaffed, all sexual fluids drained from his body, and he would slowly walk back to the showers, and then return to the locker rooms to get a clean towel from the stack of towels there, to dry off, get dressed, and leave. No, on slow days, one sometimes has to be the early bird to get the thick juicy worm that enters the steam room.

But this particular day was not slow, so Ricardo simply watched the man who entered the steam room, feeling his way along the wall. The man was not young, not particularly old, not particularly fat, but not muscular. His hair was not blond but not brown. In other words, there was nothing particularly distinctive about the man. Ricardo simply noticed him come into the steam room, and watched him feel his way along the walls, grope his way through the steam room and down into the dark room corridors. Had it not been for the events that happened later, Ricardo would have forgotten about the man altogether.

I should explain the dark room corridors. In this particular bathhouse, the steam room is designed like the hub of a wheel, dimly lit by blue lights, with the aforementioned large concrete steps for sitting and resting. Running off of this hub, like bent spokes on a wheel, are various corridors, also filled with steam, though not quite as hot as the steam room. But these corridors are not lit, and they twist and turn, forming a labyrinth, some leading to rooms with concrete benches, some just folding back in on themselves. It's quite possible for newcomers to get lost in the twists and turns of these corridors, but eventually they all lead back to either the steam room or to clearly marked exit doors. But as mentioned, these corridors are completely pitch black, and they provide the perfect place for the shy, the old, the ugly, the fat, and the adventuresome to wander, to fondle, to suck, to fuck, and to abandon each other when done, all in total anonymity. They also provide some relief from the heat of the steam room, although there are also cool showers in the steam room, off to one side, where the overheated who wish to remain in the steam room can cool down. Normally, everyone who comes to the bathhouse wanders down the dark room corridors several times during a visit, just for the thrill, because... again, since we're being honest, my friends... there is nothing quite like the ghastly thrill of being fondled or sucked, being taken, as it were, in complete darkness by a total stranger, a stranger whom you cannot see at all. It's a type of submission, isn't it? Or a type of dominance, depending on your preference.

But returning to the nondescript man: as mentioned, Ricardo had seen him come into the steam room and feel his way down one of the darkroom corridors, and Ricardo thought no more about it, as he was distracted by the next person who entered—a young lad, slight of build, with hardly any hips, completely shaven, so that his cock and balls hung out like Christmas ornaments on his crotch. This was more to Ricardo's liking...

It was not until later, perhaps thirty minutes or so, that Ricardo saw the nondescript man again. Ricardo had left the steam room to wander around other corridors of the bathhouse when he passed the man coming the other way. At first he did not recognize the man, but then he remembered that this was the same man he had seen earlier in the steam room, feeling his way along the wall, and the reason Ricardo recognized him was because the man was doing the same exact thing in the hallway—that is, the man was feeling his way along the wall by holding his left hand up against the wall for guidance and walking slowly along, holding his right hand up in front of him in case he encountered any person or obstacle. But this hallway was well-lit, easy to see, so his walking that way made no sense. Ricardo looked more closely at the nondescript man's face. His eyes were half-closed; his head slightly tilted back, his mouth slightly open. Ricardo realized that the man was blind, or at least severely visually impaired.

How odd, Ricardo thought—a blind man in the gay bathhouse. But why not? In the dark rooms he would be as sighted as anyone—the blind fondling the blind. But how did he get here? By taxi, Ricardo assumed, and then he must have tapped his way to the door. Ricardo visualized the man with his white cane, tapping to the bathhouse door, paying his fee, tapping his way to the locker room. Maybe he was a regular, Ricardo thought. Why not? Blind gay men need relief too. And then, once again, the thought of the man left Ricardo's mind as he wandered into one of the non-steam room corridors, looking to see who he might find.

It was only later, perhaps another twenty minutes or so, that Ricardo learned more about this blind man. Ricardo had stepped into the Turkish heat room—the dry heat room—and was sitting on a wooden bench just relaxing with several other men, when the blind man wandered in. One of the other men on the bench, a big man, took a liking to the blind man and approached him from behind, rubbed the blind man's back, rubbed his ass, and reached around and fondled his cock. Then the big man stepped in closer behind the blind man and began to try and insert his erect cock into the blind man's ass.

Fucking in bathhouses was something that Ricardo usually avoided, due to the threat of AIDS, or SIDA as it is known in this country. Many of the men who did fuck in the bathhouse carried condoms and small tubes of lube, and there were condom dispensers situated around the bathhouse for those who needed them. But Ricardo also knew that some men simply did not use condoms. They stimulated themselves until they were erect, strapped a cock ring on to stay erect, lubed their cocks up and went looking for an available ass, any ass, that would let them in. Such conduct was considered dangerous, but it did happen. Ricardo could not see whether this big man had a condom on or not, but clearly there was some difficulty in getting his cock inside the blind man. Maybe he wasn't lubed up enough... but the blind man began to grunt, and it was clear that the cock was not going in.

It was the grunt that drew Ricardo's attention, because it was not the throaty grunt of a regular man— it had the back-of-the-throat sound that only the deaf make, because the deaf have no reference to what a normal grunting sound is like, and since all language and all sound is imitative, their grunts do not sound normal. And then Ricardo began to listen closely to the blind man's grunts and suddenly he realized that this man was not only blind, but he was deaf and mute as well. He couldn't speak; he couldn't hear; and he couldn't see. And evidently he did not want to be fucked in the ass because the grunts became louder and stranger and more painful until finally the big man pulled away, letting the blind man go, and the blind man felt his way out of the Turkish room, arms extended to find the door.

How odd, how strange, Ricardo thought. Earlier, he held a bit of admiration for the blind man, because he had imagined him talking to his sighted friends, confessing that he was gay, asking them to bring him for the first time to the gay bathhouse where he introduced himself to the staff and took a tour, memorizing all the rooms in his mind's eye, so that he could return by himself on a regular basis in the future and find much needed physical relief. Because of that fantasy, Ricardo had been admiring the blind man's courage; but now his opinion had changed. It had changed because as he listened to the man grunt instead of making words in the Turkish room, as he stared carefully at the man's face, he realized that this creature was not normal, not fully cognizant. Either he was limited and impaired by his handicap or he was also mentally deficient, but it made no difference as to the cause, because the result was the same. And as this creature fumbled and felt his way out of the Turkish room, Ricardo was overcome by such a sense of sadness, of pity, not only for this creature, but for all the blind creatures, including himself, in the bathhouse.

There are many different kinds of men who come to bathhouses, from famous actors and university professors to high school dropouts. It's a true melting pot of flesh. And over the years, Ricardo had been with different men of different educational levels, some of them rather stupid but perhaps good looking, or good looking enough in the dim light. But it's one thing to fuck someone who's not that bright—after all, they're there for the same reason you are—and quite another thing to fuck a creature so impaired that they cannot seem to communicate.

Blind, deaf and mute, born in shadows, perhaps living in idiocy or simply deprived of sufficient stimuli to develop, and then coming to this place, where his ass might be fucked or his cock sucked or maybe he might find a corner to sit where he would suck any cock that was shoved in his mouth by someone who had no idea that he was being sucked off by someone so impaired... The image of this creature being taken by another man, simply being fucked like a pig and abandoned, took all the sexiness out of sex, all of the pride out of gay pride.

And so Ricardo was left sitting in the semi-darkness, not knowing who or what this creature was; how this creature first came to the bathhouse; how he survived; or how he would find his way through life.

Chapter 2:   THE BATHHOUSE POPE

This bathhouse of which I speak, my friends, is located in La Chorrera, a fairly large tropical city in the central valley, surrounded by low mountains. It is the largest bathhouse in La Chorrera, but then again, it is the only bathhouse in La Chorrera. A few days after first seeing the blind deaf-mute, Ricardo, who lived in the neighboring town of Villa Rosario, had returned to La Chorrera to meet up with his friend Miguel at the bathhouse. Ricardo was sitting with Miguel in the hot tub and had just finished telling Miguel about the blind deaf-mute.

"Oh yes, my friend," Miguel was saying, "I've seen him here too. Not often, but once or twice before. A very strange fellow."

"Is he retarded?" Ricardo asked.

"I do not know," Miguel replied. "Besides, how could anyone tell? You can't talk with him. He wanders these hallways like a silent ghost. But I think he is aware that he is different. He never sits in the steam room—he always goes into the dark rooms where no one can see him. I think he walks around there for hours waiting for someone to blow him, or maybe he goes there to suck off anyone who can't see him. Who knows?"

"Maybe he can make out light and darkness," Ricardo suggested.

"Maybe...I don't know...but did you notice his body? Except for the hair on his head, he is completely hairless, and not from shaving. I touched him one time and his skin feels strange. It is unnaturally smooth, like a baby's skin... no hair."

"Odd," Ricardo said, "how very odd."
Just then Jared walked by the hot tub. Ricardo looked at him. A nice looking lad, Ricardo thought. Thin, long muscles like a swimmer, a nice cock, a nice face. Jared walked by without making eye contact and headed towards the steam room.

"He's cute," Ricardo said.

"Oh that's Jared," said Miguel, "a sweet boy. He's a photographer. Works in Santa Rita. I've seen his work—he's quite good."

"Hmmm, he is cute," Ricardo repeated. "Maybe I'll wander off to the steam room and meet him."

"Oh," said Miguel, "you need to be careful. He is VIH positive."

"Oh dear," said Miguel, "that's a shame. How do you know?"

"One of the waiters in my restaurant told me. I get all the gay gossip from them. No, Jared is VIH positive. He takes medicine for it of course, but still, if you go with him, you need to be careful."

"I'll pass," said Ricardo. "Why take the risk?"

"Well, there's very little risk, my friend, if you're careful."

"I'm always careful," Ricardo replied.

*   *   *

While Ricardo and Miguel continued talking, Jared entered the steam room and took a seat on one of the concrete steps. He sat slightly away from the other men sitting on the other steps and made no eye contact with them. But he picked one of the narrow steps to sit on, one which supported his back yet allowed him to sit right at waist level and just a few inches away from anyone who walked by. He undid his towel and began playing with himself. A few men walked into the steam room, but walked on by—they were headed for the dark room corridors. But the next man who walked in paused and watched Jared stroke his cock. Jared's cock was getting hard now. The man, an older man, but still nice-looking, took a step toward Jared. Jared kept stroking himself with his left hand, but reached up with his right hand and took the man's cock and guided it into his mouth and began to suck. The man's cock started off with that soft skin feel that flaccid cocks have, spongy, soft, smooth, sweet—a feel that Jared loved. Then the man's cock began to swell in Jared's mouth. Jared liked that as well. Jared liked sucking cock more than anything in the world, even better than cumming himself. He loved how the cock would harden itself, transforming from a soft wilted flower into a hard and demanding hammer. He loved the feeling of a stiff cock jammed against the back of his throat; he loved running his tongue over the smooth head, feeling how it flanged out before curving down to the shaft; he loved the ripply feel of the shaft with its veins; he loved the way it throbbed in his mouth as men became more excited; he especially loved it when men lost control, grabbing his head and fucking his mouth harder, shoving the cock as far down his throat as it could go before the cock gave a shudder and squirted hot cum against the back of his throat. He loved the large loads of cum the best, cum that came out fast and strong, sometimes filling his mouth so fast that it shot out the corners of his mouth before he could swallow it all.

Men usually liked to pull out of his mouth after they had cum, but Jared would reach around and grab their ass and hold them in, so that he could suck every last drop of cum out of their cocks, so that he could feel the cock start to soften and shrink, so that the intense ticklish feeling of still being sucked would be more than the men could stand and they would have to push against his shoulders to pull out... pull out and stumble into the darkness saying, "thank you, thank you, thank you" as they left.

Jared didn't always love sucking cock so much. He had been an ass man for years. He had loved taking it up the ass, being dominated by some stranger in the bathhouse, or by someone he had met in a gay bar and taken home. He used to use laxatives and enemas everyday to clean himself out before going out to find sex. In those days, when he went to the bathhouse, he would use a small squeeze-bottle filled with lubricant, like a miniature turkey baster, to lube up the inside of his ass before he stepped into the steam room. That way any partner could simply bend him over the concrete steps and fuck him right there. And Jared didn't like condoms, so he never used them. All of that coincided with his meth use, of course. He had been hooked on crystal, and it drove his sexual desires through the ceiling. Even after cumming three or four times during an afternoon at the bathhouse, he would stay long into the night, just letting other men fuck him, his own cock being quite exhausted and dead, but the other men didn't care—they just wanted a young ass to fuck, and Jared was just the young ass for the job.

All that of course was years ago, before he caught VIH, before his world came crashing down, before the suicide attempts, before his hospitalization, before he got clean and found Jesus. For many years now, he had accepted being VIH positive as his penance, his cross to bear. And thank God, there was medicine which kept his infection from growing into SIDA. And thank God, he had gotten clean and had made his peace with God. And Jared's peace with God meant that he no longer let men fuck him in the ass, nor did he fuck anyone else in the ass. He didn't even let other men suck him to orgasm. But his peace with God did allow him to suck other men off. His doctor had explained to Jared that as long as he took his medication and as long as he didn't have a cut or sores in his mouth, the other men who came in his mouth had a negligible risk of catching the VIH infection from Jared. And so Jared forged his peace with God, went to mass every Sunday and came to the bathhouse every Wednesday, and sucked as many cocks as he could, giving pleasure to any man who needed it, no matter how old, fat, lame, unattractive or repugnant they might be. It was like the Pope washing the feet of the sinners, Jared believed. Yes, Jared was the Pope of the bathhouse, washing away the sins of the sinner with his mouth and tongue, offering consecration by his lips, sucking the weakness of the flesh out of each man, so they could go forth in the world and do God's work.

Once or twice, maybe more, Jared had sucked off the blind deaf-mute, always in the darkest corner of the darkroom corridors, where the blind man would glide along the walls he had memorized, until he found Jared leaning against the wall. And Jared would recognize the blind deaf-mute by touch, feeling his soft round hairless body, and Jared would get down on one knee and suck that hairless cock until the blind man grunted that eerie guttural cry and small drops of cum would fall into Jared's mouth. And then the blind man would glide away, and Jared would stand up, and wait for the next sinner to step into the confession box.

Chapter 3: ESTEBAN

At some point during every visit to the bathhouse, Jared would reach a point of satiation. Sometimes it was after only an hour or two, other times after three or four hours, depending on how many men he had sucked. But there would always come a point where he had had enough—a point at which he felt tired, or rather, felt a feeling of being finished, of having sucked enough cocks, having swallowed enough cum. His mouth would be tired; his jaw might ache a bit, and his stomach would be full. He knew it would soon be time to get dressed and leave the bathhouse. Often times he might not have cum yet himself, although he usually tried to time his orgasms to happen with one of the lattermost men and not the earlier ones. But it all depended on whether he would be lucky enough to find a buenísimo cock—one that somehow got him excited enough to want to cum. It didn't have to be a large one, or one of any particular shape or girth. It was more the person to whom it was attached. If the man had a certain quality, a quality that made Jared feel that "this could be someone I could love," then Jared would stroke himself harder as he sucked and try to cum just as the man was cumming in his mouth, while he pretended that they knew each other, that they loved each other, that they were long-time lovers.

But those special moments did not happen often, and usually Jared simply reached a point of having had enough, of wanting to go home. And then it was his habit to sit quietly on one of the benches outside the steam room, his towel wrapped around him, just sitting quietly and thinking...or rather, feeling. And what he was invariably feeling was sadness, because every Wednesday, after his afternoon of holy servitude was done, the same thought would always form in Jared's head, and that sad, sad thought was: "I'll never find anyone." For despite all the medication, and his almost undetectable viral count, Jared still had VIH, and his ability to date, to even introduce himself to others, to make any kind of contact was forever inhibited, curtailed, and quashed by the knowledge that a normal love relationship was out of his reach. The doctors and his friends had all tried to tell him otherwise years ago, of course, but Jared knew better, and as his friends drifted away one by one, it only confirmed the truth. And so Jared constructed his life around his work, his church, and his Wednesday afternoons at the bathhouse. For here, at least for a few hours, he could let himself imagine what love would be like, remember what it had once been like, and mourn what it would never be like for him again.

And so, at the end of every Wednesday afternoon, Jared would sit quietly on the wooden bench outside of the steam room door, feeling sad, and saying a little prayer to God for the courage to get through another week, and he would remind himself that his peace with God at least allowed him this weekly bounty, this weekly servitude, this weekly penance in this beautiful bathhouse.

And as he was sitting there on this particular afternoon, lost in his thoughts, Jared did not notice Esteban walk past him and enter the steam room.

This was only Esteban's second time at this bathhouse. He was still scoping the place out, checking the type of men who came here, checking the type of security cameras at the front counter, and especially checking out the placement of the private rooms. So far, he was pleased with this particular bathhouse. The security cameras were mounted high in the entrance hall—that meant that if he wore a hat, it would obscure his face. Plus, this bathhouse had private rooms scattered in various places throughout, not built in rows like in other bathhouses. Esteban needed privacy for his particular preference of love-making. And more importantly, the inside of the private rooms only used a cabin latch as a lock, that is, on the inside of each private room there was a simple metal hook stapled to the door that would fit into an eye screw on the opposite door jamb. When an amorous duo or trio of men would enter the room for privacy, they would simply insert the metal hook into the eyelet to secure the door closed. It wasn't designed for security—only to keep the door closed while they had sex and prevent someone from opening it.

Esteban preferred this type of latch above all others because, years ago, he had fashioned a small curved wire device from a coat hanger that allowed him to latch the door from the outside as he left the room. That way, whomever he left in the private room would not be disturbed for many, many hours, perhaps not until the next day, long after Esteban had left the bathhouse, and long after Esteban had left the city.

For Esteban liked having sex with men; he especially liked to seduce them into a private room, and then, once inside the private room, to tease them with more sex, to weaken them by performing increasingly forbidden things to their bodies; to gently beguile them to letting him tie their hands; and then to mount them from behind; to ease his lubricated cock into their assholes; and then to fuck them, slowly at first; then harder; then harder still; and then at the last minute, he'd force their face deep into the pillow of the bed where they could not scream and could not breathe, and he'd fuck them hard while they asphyxiated and died. For it was in death's final struggle that Esteban found the true total pleasure of fucking— the holding down of the unwilling victim, their useless struggle against Esteban's superior strength, and most of all, the extreme clenching of their rectal muscles as they died just as he came, shooting hot cum into their poor wretched asses, finishing off the last eight or nine strokes into a lifeless corpse. That was pure heaven to Esteban.

He had found over the years that it was extremely easy to kill someone, that if they were properly positioned on their stomachs, if the pillow on which their head rested was nice and fluffy, if their hands were incapacitated, if the full weight of his body was on them, if they were already out of breath from sex, if they were older, if they were overheated from hours in the steam room, if they were on any medication, that it took so little to simply turn their head quickly with both of his hands so that it was directly in the pillow and then press his upper body weight on both his forearms against the back of their neck and hold them down for five or ten seconds or so. That's all the time it took for them to pass out. Oxygen is such a moment-by-moment need, that when a person is deprived of it unexpectedly, without time to prepare, that by the time they've missed two or three breaths of air, they black out, and Esteban only had to maintain his weight on their neck another two or three minutes until they were completely dead. The interesting thing, he had noticed years earlier, was that even then they were passed out and could no longer struggle against him, that their bodies still fought the act of dying. That's when the rectal muscles really began to spasm, clenching his cock as if they were grasping a helping hand reaching in to save them from drowning. And Esteban would fuck them all the harder then, driving his cock deeper and deeper into their ass, without any remorse, harder and harder, until their rectal death grip coaxed every squirt of cum out of him.

It did not bother him that he was leaving behind DNA evidence, because he knew that his cum would probably be mixed with the cum of other men who had fucked that same person that day. Therefore, any DNA could not be used as conclusive evidence against him. But it would never even come to that, because Esteban also knew the truth about bathhouses—that people died there all the time, and the bathhouses covered up these deaths, and the police never investigated these deaths, and the gay community didn't talk about these deaths, and family members never asked any questions when they learned where the death occurred. There were so many older men who came to bathhouses, older men who then spent too long in the heat of the steam room or the dry heat room, men who usually took Cialis or Viagra and then often—foolishly or inadvertently—inhaled a nitrate popper at the bathhouse, triggering a sudden drop in blood pressure that resulted in death; or so many other men who were chronic users of coke or meth that their hearts would give out just at the peak moment of sexual activity. (In fact, my friends, there are thousands of men all over the world who have permanently sworn off bathhouses after some lover died purple-faced in their arms.) Death is common in bathhouses, and Esteban knew that all bathhouses over the years developed professional relationships with a core group of doctors, coroners, police departments, morticians and hospitals. No one wanted any trouble. As long as there were no signs of violence, it was in everyone's interest to agree that the poor pitiful deceased had had a heart attack, or had accidently overdosed, or both.

Esteban knew all this, and counted on these things. But he was also very careful. He wore a hat when he checked into the bathhouse, to obscure his face from the surveillance cameras at the entrance. He never used his real name. He carried fake ID in case the bathhouse required ID. He always paid in cash. He never talked with anyone inside the bathhouse nor did anything to make anyone remember him. He would stay quietly by himself in the shadows, just watching the men cruise by. He only picked older men, ones who had that haunted look of lonely solitary gay men, handsome ones yes, but ones who weren't physically strong enough to fight back. Plus, Esteban wouldn't pick them up right away—once he spotted a promising-looking victim, he would wait until he saw that they had had a couple of sexual encounters, so that their mouths or rectums might contain traces of other men's DNA either from semen or saliva. Then he would approach them in the shadows, play with them, getting their cocks engorged, and then play with their assholes a bit, to see if they liked ass play, to see if they would like being fucked in the ass. Esteban knew that if a man allowed him to put his finger in their ass in the steam room, they would let him put his whole cock up there in the private room. When he had aroused a suitable victim, he would then invite them back to the private room he had preselected. Once inside the room, with the door latched, the drama would begin in earnest: the seduction of the bride, the soft caresses, the careful grooming away of all defenses, like a cook tenderly seasoning the meat, the kisses, the teasing—because Esteban didn't want them to cum too quick—he had to arouse them to the point where they wanted him so much they surrendered control to him—he had to gain their trust through sucking and kissing, and then when they were aroused, by his rimming of their asshole while they lay on their stomachs, then lubricating their assholes with his finger, and then the all important convincing them to let him tie their hands. He would start that process by gently holding their hands down while kissing them, getting them used to being gently dominated, then holding their whole arms down while they lay on their backs and he straddled them, gently forcing his cock into their mouths. By the time they were on their stomachs with Esteban licking their assholes and thrusting his tongue into their ass, they had usually completely surrendered to the bliss of sexual domination. It was a simple matter to ease both of their arms behind their backs, overlapping the wrists, and hold the wrists there while he continued to rim them and push his finger into their ass. From there, Esteban only had to undo the thin Velcro strap he kept around his wrist, tie it gently around their wrists, and then start to lube up their asses with lubricant from a tube he carried in a small bag. By this point, they trusted him. By the time someone is lubing up your ass, you have already totally submitted to them. Then he would lube up his cock, already hard from just the anticipation, climb on top of them, pushing their legs apart, and start to push his cock into their ass. Then the real fun began. Then he could let the real Esteban out.

He kept a small bottle of Amyl Nitrate in his small bag, a bottle that had a pop-top with a hinge, so that he could pop it open with the thumb of one hand. Sometimes he would reach into the bag, grab the bottle, pop the top, and force it under the nose of his victim while he was fucking them. Most older men in bathhouses took Cialis, Viagra, or Levitra to help them maintain their erections, and many of them didn't know of the lethal combination of those drugs with Amyl Nitrate. Some didn't notice the smell of the bottle that he held under their nose. The ones who did recognize the smell and turned their heads away to avoid inhaling, well, they simply aided Esteban in positioning their heads face down in the pillow. Esteban always left the bottle of Amyl Nitrate next to the bodies as further evidence of the accidental nature of what befell his victims.

And after they were dead, Esteban would carefully arrange their bodies to look as natural as possible, pull the sheet up over their torso as if they were napping, and use his towel to wipe any areas where he might have left fingerprints, including the bottle of Amyl Nitrate. Then he would listen at the door to make sure no one was in the corridor outside the room, step outside, and use the wire tool from the his little bag to latch the door from the outside, then head off to shower and check out of the bathhouse.

Of course, he would also remove the locker key from the dead man's wrist, and help himself to the dead man's wallet back in the locker room, taking only the cash, never the credit cards. Then he would return to the private room, flip open the latch with his wire hook, slip the locker key back on the man's wrist, relatch the door and leave. If the bathhouse was real busy, so that it took him longer to leave the private room because he had to wait until the corridor was empty, then he would skip the theft. Not worth the risk of being seen. But most of the time, he could pick up an extra two or three hundred dollars this way. Most patrons of bathhouses like to pay cash—no point in leaving a trail of credit card receipts.

And once he had checked out of the bathhouse, he would never return, at least not for a year. He would go back to whatever hostel or cheap motel he was staying in and check out of there as well, and catch a bus out of town, heading off to the next city on his list—a circuit of cities that spanned several countries, cities that he mapped out over the years, ones that had a strong gay subculture, ones that had at least one or two bathhouses.

But on this visit, his second, Esteban was only scouting out the bathhouse. He was methodical in his work. He was learning the layout of the bathhouse, the pattern of the darkened corridors, where the emergency exits were, the kind of clientele they had, and the security (or lack thereof) they had. Esteban was only there to memorize the layout. He glanced at Jared as he walked by, but quickly dismissed him as too young to target. He didn't want anyone who could fight back, because he could not leave any bruises—bruises would raise suspicions, and suspicions were not good. So Esteban walked by Jared and continued with his mental mapping of the bathhouse, and walked into the steam room.

Chapter 4:   AARON

Aaron liked to get to the bathhouse early in the afternoon on Thursdays. Well, to be honest, "liked to" is perhaps the wrong phrase. He "needed to" get to the bathhouse early on Thursdays, because it was the only way he could spend time there without being detected by his wife. Over the years he had worked out a schedule. His wife regularly worked late on Thursdays at the school where she was the principal. Thus, she did not get home that day until 7 p.m. Normally, she was home by 5 p.m. and Aaron had dinner ready for her when she walked in the door. His job ended at 3:30 every afternoon, which left him just enough time to drive home and prepare dinner. He was never sure how he had ended up with this particular domestic task— he didn't enjoy cooking, but his wife enjoyed it less, and somehow over the years, it became a custom, a duty, an obligation, and an expectation that he would have a hot meal waiting for her. She was always very prompt and if the meal was a few minutes late, she would make some subtle comment about how hard she worked. Left unsaid, but implied in her comments, would be the fact that she earned more money than Aaron, and that this small service of his really wasn't too much to expect. Also left unsaid was the fact of her eating disorder—she had a whole list of food allergies and intolerances, including lactose, gluten, nuts, soy, eggs, and shellfish. Thus, she normally only ate a small salad for lunch at her school and was always hungry when she got home, hungry and cranky. It was probably the fact that she got so cranky when she was hungry that, over the years, shaped Aaron's habit of preparing dinner for her—he simply didn't want to listen to her bitching. If he fed her immediately when she arrived home, she was usually relatively tolerable for the rest of the evening.

It wasn't that Aaron didn't love his wife...well, again, to be honest, Aaron didn't love his wife. But they served each other's purpose, and that particular purpose was the appearance of marriage. They had married thirty years ago, when each was under intense pressure by either family or job to be married. It was a different time back then, and the social pressure on both effeminate young men and ambitious professional women to be married was overwhelming. But it was a totally sexless marriage, partially by agreement—they had discussed it some before marriage—but mostly by circumstance and habit. Once they had established separate bedrooms during the first three months of marriage, they simply never slept together again for the next three decades. But that didn't stop the evolution of some very married traditions, such as her developing into a domineering wife and his regression into a henpecked husband. As she rose in her chosen profession, and he stagnated in his job, she took on the role of boss at home as well as at work.

But, as mentioned, on Thursdays, Aaron had that extra sliver of time, that precious respite from his regimented life, almost two full hours, time he could steal from the Gods and shoehorn undetected into his daily routine—that blessed sanctuary when he could simply be himself, and by "be himself" I mean, be gay. For Aaron had been gay all his life. He realized it young and enjoyed it. He had started sucking off other boys as far back as sixth grade, before any of them were even sexually mature enough to ejaculate. The other boys grew out of it—for them it was either a phase of growing up, or their parents beat it out of them if they discovered it. But Aaron stayed with it. As a teenager, he would spend his Saturdays at the bus stop near the movie theatre downtown. If a bus came by, he would pretend it wasn't his bus—that he was waiting for another bus. But he wasn't waiting for a bus at all. He was waiting for some older gay man to drive by, slow down, circle the block, ease up to the curb, wave at Aaron as if he knew him, roll down his window and say, "Need a lift?" and Aaron would nod and hop in the passenger side. To any of the other people waiting for the bus, it simply looked as if a neighbor of Aaron's was doing him a favor and giving him a ride home. But that, of course, was not the case. It was simply the subterfuge that had developed, as such subterfuges do, in the gay subculture of the town where

Aaron had grown up, as such diverse subterfuges always develop in all gay communities, whether it's the particular corner of a particular park where gay men cruise, or the particular balcony of a particular theatre where gay men wait. Such secret places and patterns are normal in every city throughout the world. And in Aaron's hometown, the pattern was simple: a gay man, usually an older gay man, would offer the teenage Aaron a ride, and moments after Aaron got in the car and the man was driving away from the bus stop, the man would say, "Do you need to get right home?" and Aaron would say no, and the man would drive to a particular secluded spot, sometimes a rural road, sometimes behind an abandoned factory, but usually to a spot in the woods. There would be some small talk along the way, but that was simply an indirect way for the man to reassure himself that Aaron was sophisticated enough to know what was going on, because when they got to the secluded spot, the man would usually put his hand on Aaron's leg and ask something like, "Have you ever been with a man before?" to which Aaron would simply nod his head yes, which was a sufficient agreement for the man to unzip Aaron's pants, pull out his adolescent cock, take one last look around, and then bend down to suck Aaron. In such encounters, there was no foreplay, no "lovemaking" as such. There was just the quick sucking, the "blow and go" as it was known in the community. The man would suck, and Aaron would cum quickly, as adolescent boys usually do. But then it always came as a surprise to the driver when Aaron would tuck his cock back into his pants, and reach over and unzip the older man's pants, pull out their man-sized cock and go down on them. Most pedophiles did not expect their victim to be so active. But as mentioned, Aaron knew he was gay, and he enjoyed sucking. He especially loved the big cocks of the older men, the ones that filled his mouth with hot flesh and then with hot cum.

When he got older, almost twenty, an older college professor introduced him to the pleasures of ass fucking. He had to work at it for almost six months, but the professor was patient and a good teacher. Aaron started off using small dildos, teaching his ass to relax, then working his way up, over a period of months, to the larger dildos. Finally came the day when the professor was able to get his cock all the way into Aaron's tight ass and fuck him, and to Aaron's amazement, Aaron came just as the professor came, without touching his cock. The fucking seemed to reach some orgasmic point deep in his ass that gave him a much more intense involuntary orgasm than he ever had just by masturbating or being sucked off. From that point on, Aaron was hooked. He was born to be a submissive, a bottom, a little femboy. He started dressing up in women's clothes whenever he could, but he was never passable, so he never went out in public dressed as a woman. It was simply his private pleasure.

He had once told his wife about this, before they were married. But she was adamant that she didn't ever want to see that when she was in the house. However, she didn't care what he wore when she was not at home. And her wardrobe was extensive. And they never talked about it again. The other agreement they had (well, to be honest, it wasn't so much an agreement as her demand) was that he was never to go public with his gayness, never go to gay bars or flaunt a gay boyfriend, or be seen purchasing gay videos, etc. And since they lived more or less on her salary, Aaron complied. But Aaron did not consider the bathhouse a public place; after all, there was a big sign in the entrance way that said "private club—members only," although the cost of the daily admission fee or "membership" was minimal. And thus, as the years rolled by, he maintained a regular habit of getting to the bathhouse every Thursday afternoon for exactly two hours where he would wrap the towel around him and pretend it was a skirt, and prance up and down the corridors looking for dominant man to take him, to fuck him, to lube up his ass and drill him hard, and make him cum.

And on this particular Thursday afternoon, Aaron entered the bathhouse right on schedule through the unmarked side door that all the customers used; he paid his fee and got a locker key, a towel, and sandals; he stripped down and stowed his clothes neatly in the locker; wrapped the towel around him and went into the bathroom and inserted a wad of lubricant deep into his ass with his finger, using up the entire tiny tube of lubricant that he had just purchased from the front counter; and then he went and showered quickly, and started cruising up and down the twisting corridors outside of the steam room. Aaron rarely went into the steam room. It made him too hot, frizzled his hair (a potential give-away to his wife), and besides, most of the tops who were looking for anal sex were cruising the corridors outside the steam room, near where the private rooms were.

Cruising in the bathhouse was not really that different than cruising in any hetero singles bar, except that every ritual is condensed down to its most elemental form. Men would walk around and around the various hallways, and when they saw someone they liked, they would circle back to pass them again, but this time try to make some eye contact. If there was eye contact, there might be a smile. If both smiled then things accelerated faster. But in any case, one would approach the other. Usually the more dominant man would reach out and gently stroke the other man's nipple or arm, sometime reach down and run his hand over the front part of the other man's towel. The more submissive man, if he was interested, would simply place an arm around the other man's waist or touch his arm and let his touch linger. It is the lingering touch that always indicates sexual interest, be it in the gay bathhouse, the singles bar, or the after church social. Once both men had touched each other, there would be a bit of conversation, because anal sex requires some agreements, some boundaries. The conversation would be more like a code than a conversation with phrases like, "I like to top," "Do you use condoms?" or "Do you have lube?" It might finally end up with "Would you like to go to a room for a bit and play?" At this point, the two men would adjourn to the nearest available room.

On this particular Thursday, Aaron had already been there over an hour and a half and was not having much luck. One man had fucked him but came right away.

Another man had tried to fuck him but couldn't get hard. Aaron knew that many men were nervous in the bathhouse so he was always kind to those who had trouble getting hard. Thus it was that Aaron was back out walking the dim corridors, hoping that he could find someone before his time ran out, someone who would fuck him good. He ratcheted up his feminine strut, hoping to attract someone who really liked slim femboys.

Esteban had been watching Aaron for almost 30 minutes, saw him disappear into a private room with one man and emerge ten minutes later, watched him walk up and down the corridors, obviously cruising. Aaron was close to fitting the bill for Esteban. He was slight of build; he had a tight-looking little ass that would probably be a good fuck; and he had that little fag walk that needed to be extinguished forever. He wasn't quite as old as Esteban liked, but he didn't look like he would be able to put up much of a fight. So Esteban continued to sit on his little bench in the dark corner and watched Aaron flit back and forth. Finally Esteban decided to make his move. The next time Aaron pranced by, Esteban stood up and followed him. As he got closer behind him, Esteban extended his hand and cupped Aaron's ass cheek. Even through the towel, Esteban could feel how small and round it was, and that excited him. Aaron however, had been aware of Esteban coming up behind him, and so, feeling the touch on his ass, he did not stop walking, but slowed down a bit and turned slightly to see Esteban.

"Hello, sailor," quipped Esteban. "Going my way?"

"That depends," said Aaron, "on how far you're going."

"I normally like to go all the way," Esteban said, giving his most charming smile.

"Do tell," said Aaron.

"Uh huh."

"No, I mean, do tell me, what would you do?" Aaron asked.

"Oh, well... first, I would like to take off that unnecessary towel, and then get you real hot." Esteban stepped closer. "And then I would suck you some, just to get you hard, but then I would rim that gorgeous ass of yours. You do like to be rimmed don't you? And then I would lube you up and fuck the life out of you."

Aaron stopped walking and looked at Esteban. The words were right but there was something that he did not like about Esteban. The smile was too nice; the tone of voice just a bit too sincere. There was a clock high up on the wall and Aaron glanced at it. He really only had ten minutes left before he needed to shower again, change back into his clothes and get home to cook dinner. He looked sadly down the darkened hall and then back at the clock, then he bit his lip and decided that this opportunity had just come along too late—that he wouldn't have enough time to enjoy it, and besides, there was something about Esteban that put Aaron off.

He patted Esteban's arm and said, "Sorry darling, some other time. I have to get going." And then Aaron turned and walked away, leaving Esteban standing there a little surprised. Surprised and angry. He had watched that little slut prance up and down the hallway for over half an hour. Fuck! Now he would have to spend another hour scoping someone else out, making another selection. Plus, that little slut had looked right at his face. He had a good mind to bash that little prick tease's head in and dump his body in a private room without fucking him. Esteban looked around for something to grab, but there was nothing except the dimly lit hallway. He tried to calm himself down. "Mustn't get angry. Mustn't get angry." He took three deep breaths, turned and walked back down the hallway and into the steam room.

Meanwhile Aaron was getting dressed in the locker room, cursing his bad luck and saying to himself, "Well, maybe next Thursday will be better."

Chapter 5:   BLIND LUCK

Esteban stepped into the steam room, still angry that Aaron had turned him down. This was Esteban's fourth trip to the bathhouse—the first two trips were simply to case the joint, to check it out. On the third visit he had hoped to find a suitable victim, but none crossed his path. This fourth trip was even more frustrating.

At the same time that Esteban was stepping into the steam room, Ricardo was stepping out of the nearby urinal. He had left Miguel sitting in the hot tub so he could go pee, and he was walking back, down the hallway back towards the hot tub. As he passed by the door of the steam room, he caught a glimpse of the blind deaf-mute man easing his way down the same hallway, going in the opposite direction, his left hand gliding along the wall. Ricardo would not have noticed him at all had it not been for the fact that he and Miguel had discussed him at length the week before, so that the blind deaf-mute's gestures and odd way of walking down the hallway (or rather, feeling his way down the hallway) were etched into Ricardo's mind. Ricardo paused and watched the deaf-mute go up to the steam room door, run his hands along the door frame until he found the handle, open the door, and step inside. Ricardo shook his head, turned and continued walking back to the hot tub.

Ricardo and Miguel had started their visit several hours earlier by relaxing in the hot tub as usual. After various successful cruising interludes in the darkroom corridors, they had returned to the hot tub for a final soak before they would call it a day.

"You know my friend," Miguel said as Ricardo returned to the hot tub, "you must remember to drink plenty of water here. Even though we are in water, the heat dehydrates our bodies. And when you pee, you lose more fluid."

"True, I will buy a bottle of water before I leave, to drink on the bus ride home," Ricardo replied as he carefully stepped into the bubbling waters of the hot tub.

"Have you noticed, my friend," Ricardo added, "how today we have been so blessed with some interesting new younger faces, some very beautiful muchachos? It's nice to see younger men here for a change."

"I agree Miguel. It's been a delightful day."

Although Miguel was pleased to see a younger clientele in the bathhouse today, Esteban was not. As mentioned, he preferred older men, or weaker men, or little femboys, men he could dominate, and even he had noticed that there were more younger men in the bathhouse today than during his three previous visits. He must have picked a bad day, he told himself. He would just have to wait until another day. Maybe he would come back on Sunday. In many bathhouses, Sunday is often a day when lonely older men, having no family and nothing else to do, would go to the bathhouse. Yes, maybe he would simply come back this Sunday.

As Esteban sat on the concrete steps of the steam room thinking about these things, the deaf-mute moved by him. Esteban glanced up at him, and was about to dismiss him as being too young, when he noticed the particularly odd way the man was feeling his way through the room. At this point, the walls in the steam room were far apart, with concrete steps for sitting on both sides, and the deaf-mute was walking through the steam room with no wall to hug; thus he walked with both hands out in the air in front of him, palms facing forward, fingers wide apart, his hands moving like antennas to detect any obstacle, as he made his way across the open steam room area to the opposite wall where there would be a hallway to the darkroom corridors.

"He's blind!" Esteban thought to himself, "How the hell did a blind man get into the bathhouse?"

Esteban stood up and quickly walked across the steam room and down the corridor that the deaf-mute had taken. He caught up with him quickly in the part of the corridor that still had a bit of reflective light from the soft blue light of the steam room. Yes, Esteban thought, the man was younger than the normal prey, but he looked soft like a dough-boy, and not capable of any strength. Esteban rubbed the deaf-mute's shoulder, and the deaf-mute stopped walking and just stood there. Esteban moved his left hand in front of the deaf-mute's face, but there was no reaction from the deaf-mute. "He *is* blind," thought Esteban, "this is perfect." He rubbed his hand over the deaf-mute's soft hairless chest, over his protruding belly, and down to the deaf-mute's pelvis, lifting his towel, and began playing with the deaf-mute's cock. The deaf-mute started feeling Esteban's chest and shoulders, running his hands up to the side of Esteban's face, and then down to the front of Esteban's towel.

"Come with me to a room," Esteban whispered sweetly into the deaf-mute's ear. But there was no response. Esteban continued playing with the deaf-mute's cock, which started to stiffen. Clearly the man liked being touched, Esteban thought, so he repeated himself, "Amigo, come with me to my room. I will fuck you good." But still there was no response. Esteban looked at the deaf-mute's face: his head was back, eyes half-closed, mouth half-open. Esteban continued playing with the man's cock with his left hand but reached up with his right hand and snapped his fingers by the man's ear—no response. "Blind and deaf! Amazing," thought Esteban. "What a Godsend." Esteban's own cock started getting hard at the thought of tying a deaf blind man up, fucking him hard, forcing his stupid-looking face into the pillow, feeling those ass muscles grip his cock as if cum were oxygen. Esteban grabbed the deaf-mute's hand and began to lead him, gently, like a lamb to the slaughter, out of the steam room towards the private room in the furthest corner of the bathhouse. The deaf-mute simply followed along, seemingly glad to have someone take charge of him.

As they stepped out of the steam room and started down the corridor, Esteban was glad to see that there was no one in the hallway, except the old janitor pushing his cleaning cart at the far end of the hallway. Esteban guided the deaf-mute down the hallways, left then right, then finally into the private room, where he latched the door behind him.

Chapter 6: JANITOR

The janitor's name was Tacho and he had worked at the bathhouse for almost 25 years, under a succession of owners. Luis, the current owner, had bought the place ten years ago, and currently employed three janitors, but the other two janitors had only been there a few weeks. Luis had great difficulty keeping janitors. No one wanted to be known as the cum-scraper in a gay bathhouse, as the one who has to clean up, scrape up, and mop up all the bodily fluids of all the gay men who sprayed their jizz daily in the bathhouse. It seemed like every other month, Tacho had to train a new janitor. Luis not only liked Tacho but depended on him to keep the bathhouse clean and the new janitors trained.

The bathhouse opened every day at noon and closed every night at 1 a.m. Tacho showed up four days a week at 11:00 a.m. to get the bathhouse ready to open. He had Sundays through Tuesdays off because they were the slowest days at the bathhouse. That is, unless one of the other janitors didn't show up, in which case Luis would call Tacho in a panic and Tacho would faithfully show up and do an extra day's work.

The first order of business each morning was to mop the steam room and the connected darkroom corridors with bleach. That had to be done before 11:30 a.m. every morning, because it took the steam generators, which were turned off every night, thirty minutes to fill the steam room and connecting corridors with warm moist steam. A bathhouse is simply not a bathhouse without a fully functioning steam room, and the patrons who showed up exactly at noon wanted a good hot shower and a bit of steam... a bit of steam and a bit of sex... because many were on their lunch hour and didn't have time to wait for hot steam, or hot sex.

For the rest of the day, there was a strict routine that included constant laundering and bleaching of the towels and sheets; mopping the floors in the many hallways outside of the steam room; checking the PH levels in the hot tub and small swimming pool; inspecting the darkroom corridors every twenty minutes with a flashlight; picking up all the used condoms, empty tubes of lubricant, empty popper bottles, and other trash that the patrons simply tossed on the floor; and the never-ending inspection and cleaning of the private rooms which included the scraping of dried cum off the walls and floors of the private rooms. The work was not hard, but it was constant. At the end of the night, Tacho would check all the private rooms again for trash, replace any soiled sheets, and start the last load of laundry. He would leave the cashiers and Luis to count the day's receipts and go home to get a good night's sleep. There were never any breaks. Tacho guessed that was why the young workers quit so frequently—they just didn't have a work ethic. He, on the other hand, was grateful for the job, and grateful for the years of employment. He was 74 years old now, and would not be able to find a job anywhere else. So, for four days a week he showed up on time at 11 a.m. and quietly did his job.

Tacho was a small man, even smaller now with age, standing about five feet two inches even in shoes. His skin was dark and he wore dark pants and a dark long sleeve shirt to work every day. He simply blended into the darkness of the bathhouse, and most of the clients never even noticed him. He pushed his little yellow cleaning cart in front of him all day, around and around the same circuitous route, stopping at each open private room to inspect it and, if necessary, change the sheets, pick up any used condoms or other trash, mop the floors, scrape any dried cum off the walls or bed posts with a small paint-scraper he kept in his back pocket, and then to push his cart on to the next room. When he came to the steam room door, he would leave his cart outside the door, pick up his flashlight and bucket and slowly walk through every dark room corridor, picking up trash. There was so much condensed steam constantly running down the walls and floors into the drains that any spurts of cum would usually be washed away within a few minutes, but Tacho kept a look-out for any particularly slick spots that needed mopping. Occasionally someone would spill a tube of lubricant on the floor, creating a slipping hazard, and that needed to be corrected quickly.

Tacho did not think of himself as gay, but as simply old. When he first took the job 25 years ago, he was so desperate for work that he didn't care that the job was looked down upon. He simply needed a job so he could eat. He soon learned never to tell people, especially women, what he did for a living—he would tell them he was a janitor, yes—there was no shame in that—but he would never say where he worked, only that it was "an office downtown." But usually—in fact, always—when a woman he was dating found out where he worked, she would end the relationship. No woman wanted to be a cum-scraper's girlfriend. Say what you want about love, my friends, but social status plays the biggest part in the attractiveness of a mate. And, as Tacho aged, his female options became less and less. Say what you want about love, but youth plays the second biggest part in the attractiveness of a mate. And one day, about fifteen years ago, one of the clients at the bathhouse took a liking to Tacho, and pulled him into one of the private rooms, unzipped his dark trousers, and sucked him off. Tacho would have protested, would have refused, would have yelled for help, but he had been without a girlfriend for almost two years and was so lonely. And the feeling of his cock being sucked was so good that he closed his eyes, stood there silently, and let the man suck him until he came. Then, without looking at the man or saying a word, he zipped up his trousers, and went back to cleaning the hallways, pushing his little yellow cart before him. And since that time, as the girlfriends became even less and less, and eventually ceased altogether as Tacho aged and grew even shorter, he simply added another ritual to his life of rituals—every other Monday, on his day off, if Luis didn't call him to come in to work, he would show up to work anyway, "to make sure things were okay," and would take off his clothes quietly in the janitor's closet and slip into the darkest of the darkroom corridors, and wait for someone to feel their way down the hall, to find him, and suck him off. It was his only sexual release, other than masturbation. He would do this thing, then get dressed in the janitor's closet, walk by the cashier's office and tell Luis that things looked good, and head home. Sometimes, he even stayed around a bit to make sure the new janitors were doing their job correctly. Luis knew exactly what Tacho was doing, of course, but never commented on it; rather, Luis played along with the ruse, chatting amicably with Tacho on those days, thanking him profusely for being so dedicated to his job, but of course never paying him for that day's "work". Luis understood Tacho's need because, occasionally, Luis would step into the darkroom himself. Every man needs a little relief occasionally.

And ever since that fateful day, fifteen years ago, when that unknown client pulled Tacho into the private room and blew him, Tacho began to change his mind about gay men. When he had first taken the job, twenty-five years ago, he, like most good Catholics, looked down on homosexuals. He only took the job, he told himself, because it was the only alternative to starving. But he never talked with the patrons, never even made eye contact with them, never acknowledged them as people. But after that experience in the private room, Tacho's view and understanding began to change. He could no longer judge gays; in fact, he became very sympathetic towards them; and never again resented scraping cum or picking up used condoms; because he understood how non-discriminating... how non-prejudicial... how truly loving and accepting... human need really is. Say what you want about love, my friends, but need is the most powerful force on earth.

Tacho felt a special kinship with the blind deaf-mute, whose name was Ernesto. He didn't know how Ernesto got to the bathhouse, but he always liked seeing him there. Ernesto had learned his way around the place very fast and seemed to know what he was doing. He had even sucked off Tacho once or twice back in the darkrooms.

And so it was that when Esteban was holding Ernesto's hand, walking him toward the private room, that Tacho looked up and saw it and thought to himself,

"Good, I'm glad Ernesto will have some good sex tonight." Even though Tacho was a ways down the hallway, he had seen Esteban around the bathhouse the last few weeks and had noted his appearance, his muscular body, and his wolf-like eyes. "I hope he is a good lover to Ernesto", Tacho thought as he went back to his mopping.

Chapter 7:   THE UNEXPECTED

After Esteban latched the door to the private room, he had to make the blind man lie down. No one had ever taken Ernesto to one of the private rooms before—he always did his business standing in the darkroom corridors—so Ernesto wasn't sure what the protocol was. He just stood there waiting for Esteban to take the lead. Esteban placed both of his hands on the blind man's shoulders, eased him backwards to the bed and then pushed slightly on Ernesto's hip to signal that Ernesto should sit. Ernesto reached his hand out behind him and realized there was a mattress there. Once Ernesto was sitting, Esteban pressed down on Ernesto's shoulder with one hand and grabbed him under the knees with his other hand and swept his legs up so that Ernesto pivoted and lay down. Now Esteban could get to work. He rubbed his hands over Ernesto's stomach and torso, gently passing over his cock and balls, teasing him. Ernesto simply assumed that this stranger was just going to blow him and then leave, like all the others did, so he just lay there and didn't move while Esteban massaged his groin. To Esteban, this was very strange—most men would moan and rub him in return. So Esteban decided to ratchet up the sex. He climbed up the foot of the bed and bent down and began to suck Ernesto's hairless cock. He reached up under Ernesto's balls with this right hand, using his elbow to push each of Ernesto's legs apart, so he could reach further up behind Ernesto's balls and begin to massage first the soft area behind his balls, and then further up to probe Ernesto's asshole. But other than Ernesto's cock getting hard, Ernesto still didn't move. Of course, to Ernesto, this is what he thought was expected of him: to lie still and let this man do whatever he was going to do. But to Esteban, it was infuriating. *His* passion depending on his victim wanting him so much they would submit to him—that they would do anything for him. This blind fuck wasn't doing anything at all! Esteban climbed up high over Ernesto's chest, and pushed his cock into Ernesto's mouth. Ernesto opened up and accepted the cock and sucked on it as he thought he was supposed to do. Esteban grabbed both of Ernesto's arms and held them down above Ernesto's head by the wrists. Ernesto didn't mind this—he assumed it was part of this new lying-down ritual, so he didn't push his wrists back against Esteban's hands as all the other men did, as they play-acted out some resistance to the play-rape they thought they were experiencing. Ernesto just let his arms lay there limp under Esteban's grip.

"Fuck it," thought Esteban, "I'm just going to get this over with." So he pulled out of Ernesto's mouth and rolled him over onto his stomach and positioned in the center of the bed, making sure the pillow was directly under Ernesto's head. Then he got behind Ernesto again, spread his legs and began to rim his asshole.

Ernesto had had men do this to him before. He didn't mind it—it felt rather pleasurable, but he knew that it sometimes meant they were going to put something in his ass, usually a finger, but sometimes they would try to put their cock in his ass. This was something that Ernesto didn't particularly like. He didn't mind it if the man's cock was small, but if they were normal size or bigger, it hurt him, and he would normally signal with his throat sound. Then he felt the man grab both his hands and place them behind his back while continuing to rim him. Again, this whole process of lying down in the private room was new to him. Then he smelled a funny smell by his nose. He recognized it—other men had put this funny smell under his nose before, but he never knew why. It seemed to make his head spin a bit. Then he felt the man slide a finger up his ass. It went in smoothly so Ernesto knew the man had put that slippery stuff on his finger. That was ok. Ernesto didn't mind that feeling. Then he felt the man put something on his wrists—it felt like a piece of scratchy cloth. Then the man pulled his finger out of his ass and pushed his legs apart a bit further and climbed up on his back and was trying to put his cock into Ernesto's ass. He could feel that the man had that wet slippery stuff on his cock, but still, Ernesto did not want this. He knew that the man's cock would be too big from when the man had his cock in his mouth. He began to make that throat sound to tell the man no, but the man kept on trying to get his cock in.

Esteban did not expect Ernesto's ass to be so tight. He had just gotten the head of his cock in when Ernesto began to grunt. Esteban had not realized that Ernesto could make any noise—he thought mutes were totally silent. Shit, this retard was just pain all the way around! He would have to kill him first and then fuck him, so he reached up with both hands and grabbed Ernesto's head and quickly jerked it face down into the pillow then folded both his arms, one on top of the other, on the back of Ernesto's neck and pressed hard, putting all his weight onto the back of Ernesto's neck.

But while Ernesto's body was soft and round, he was not without strength, and Ernesto began to struggle, and struggle with more twisting and force than Esteban had ever expected. Sometimes the singularity of purpose of the mentally deficient gives them an unusual strength, and so it was with Ernesto. His entire body began to twist and bounce on the bed, more than Esteban could control. Esteban had not counted on this. While Esteban was muscular and very strong, Ernesto had mass and began to buck and twist on the bed. Because Esteban hadn't pried Ernesto's legs far enough apart, Esteban did not have the leverage of his pelvis against Ernesto's pelvis, and Ernesto was able to pull his knees up and raise his pelvis up on the bed. Esteban began to slide off of him. Then Ernesto was able to turn his head to the side to get air, and worse, began to grunt loudly. Esteban pulled his fist back and struck Ernesto as hard as he could in the face, on his jaw, near his mouth. Once... twice... three times! Blood formed at Ernesto's mouth, yet he continued to grunt. So Esteban wrapped his hands around Ernesto's throat and squeezed hard, and continued squeezing with all his might. He slid off of Ernesto, and stood on the floor over the head of the bed, bent over Ernesto, squeezing... squeezing. With his hands tied behind his back, Ernesto could only twist on the bed and try to kick Esteban, but he couldn't reach out and grab him. Ernesto tried to get up off the bed one last time, but then his body shuddered and went limp.

Esteban continued to squeeze Ernesto's throat for another five minutes, just to make sure this little motherfucker would never grunt again. Ernesto's face had turned blue and his eyes were wide open and bulging out of his head. Esteban could see that both eyes were a cloudy blue, the cloudy blue eyes of the blind, once alive, now quite dead.

Esteban had to pull his hands off of Ernesto's neck. Both his hands were cramped and hurt and looked like claws, and Esteban shook them to get feeling back into them. Then he looked quickly at the door, stepped over to it and listened. He heard nothing outside. He put his eye to the slit between the door from the door jamb. He saw nothing except the opposite wall. Hopefully no one heard a thing. He had picked this private room because it was the furthest away from the steam room where the men all congregated. But still, he needed to get out of there. He quickly went over to Ernesto's lifeless body and removed the Velcro strap from the man's wrists. He closed Ernesto's eyes with the edge of his hand but still his face looked ghastly, so Esteban rolled him over so he was facing the wall and covered him with a sheet. Then he took the spilled bottle of Amyl Nitrate and placed it on top of the sheet near Ernesto's head, being careful to wipe any fingerprints off of it. He stowed the Velcro strap in his little bag, wrapped his towel around him, and after listening again at the door, he opened it slowly, glanced up and down the hallway, stepped outside and closed the door, and used his little wire device to flip the inside latch into the eyelet, locking the door. He had decided to forego taking the dead man's locker key—there was no point in pressing his luck. Had that fat blob not made those grunting sounds, Esteban would have fucked his lifeless body just for spite, but he had totally botched this job and only wanted to get out of the bathhouse and out of town as fast as he could. He made his way to the locker room, changed into his street clothes quickly, turned in his key to the disinterested clerk at the desk, and stepped out into the evening air and into freedom. He had dodged another bullet. No one had seen him leave the room. There was no one in the locker room except that old janitor mopping up, and the desk clerk didn't even look at him as he checked out.

Chapter 8:   PADRES

It was many hours later, at 12:40 a.m. to be exact, when the desk clerk made the announcement over the intercom that the bathhouse would be closing in twenty minutes. This closing ritual was usually the one time each day that the intercom was used. The place had been wired over thirty years ago for an intercom to warn of police raids, but those days were long over. Now the intercom only served as the closing bell. At 12:50 a.m. the desk clerk threw the main switch that turned all the lights on in the bathhouse. There's nothing like bright lights to take all the romance out of a sex-gathering place. The few remaining men scurried to finish dressing and check out, and to step outside into the cool darkness to get away from the glaring lights. At 12:55 a.m. Tacho began making his sweeps of the dark room (now well-lit) corridors and the private rooms. But when he came to the last private room, the one way in the back corner of the bathhouse, he saw that it was locked. He put his eye to the crack between the door and the door jamb and saw what looked to be someone sleeping on the bed. "Wasn't this the same room he had seen Ernesto go into hours earlier?" he thought to himself. Well, if Ernesto had fallen asleep, he certainly would not have heard the closing announcement. So Tacho used his paint scraper to slide in-between the open slit between the door and the door jamb and flip open the inside latch. Then he stepped inside the room, walked up to the sleeping figure, and gently reached out to shake him awake.

But the touch was cold, and adrenaline instantly filled Tacho. He had seen this before, but oh no please, not Ernesto. He pulled the body over. And then he saw Ernesto's face.

Tacho ran to the front desk as fast as his frail legs could carry him, yelling at the desk clerk to call Luis. Tacho knew instinctively not to call the police until Luis arrived. Luis would decide what to do.

*   *   *

What Tacho didn't know, and what Luis didn't know, and what no one knew until later, was that Ernesto's parents were rich. When people use the phrase "justice can be bought", they usually mean that rich people can buy their way out of being held accountable for a crime. But in many parts of the world, it has the opposite meaning. In countries where law enforcement is lax to non-existent, only the rich can underwrite the investigations so that wrongdoers can be caught and held accountable. In such countries, everyone understands that if a crime occurs, the police will be untrained, understaffed, and incompetent to solve the crime, and the family must hire private investigators to dig up evidence, and then put pressure on local politicians who will in turn put pressure on prosecutors and courts to look at the evidence and bring charges against the accused. In many countries in the world—well, let's be honest, my friends—in most countries of the world, this is how justice is really financed. And such was the case in this country. So when the police showed up at the door of Ernesto's parents—Oscar and María José Pavones—with the horrible news about their son, the Pavones immediately called their friend don Fernando to hire a private investigator.

For it was true that Luis had called the police—he had to, given the look on Ernesto's face and the red and blue strangle marks on his neck. This was no overdose, no heart attack, no overheating accident. Plus, Luis had a trusted witness—Tacho—who saw Ernesto go into that room with the man who had the wolf-like eyes; and Tacho, who saw all the comings and goings in the bathhouse, never saw Ernesto again that evening until he turned his lifeless body over. Tacho was more than just an old janitor—his mind and memory were razor sharp, and Luis had trusted him for the last ten years. Tacho was Luis' eyes and ears, and saw everything that happened in the bathhouse. It was Tacho who convinced him to call the police by telling him: "You cannot keep this death quiet. Already the desk clerk has seen the body, and two guests who were just checking out heard the commotion, and they went back and saw the body. The word will get out in the community—it is probably already out because people always talk. If you do not call the police, no one will come to your business ever again because they will think it is unsafe, that you can be murdered here with impunity. You will lose your business. If you call the police and close down for two or three days, and open up, with a security guard present at the front desk, people will know that you care and will trust you, and your business will return."

Tacho's words made sense to Luis, and so, reluctantly, he called the police. And as it turned out, the first policeman who arrived, a man named Antonio, recognized that the dead man was Ernesto José Pavones, and immediately called his superiors. The dispatcher had sent Antonio to the bathhouse only because Antonio was the lowest ranking police officer on the force, and thus was assigned the late night shift, and the dispatcher had assumed this was just another overdose or heart attack at the bathhouse. But when Antonio's superiors learned who the dead man was, they sent five more officers to the scene and showed up themselves.

Don Fernando was asleep when he got the call from Oscar Pavones. But he woke up right away, for he knew how much money and influence the Pavones family had. Don Fernando was the police chief of Villa Rosario, the next town over, but he was well known in the county because he had been police chief for so many decades. The populace ascribed super sleuth abilities to him and believed he was capable of keeping brujos and evil spirits away from their town. However, don Fernando knew that his reputation was his best weapon—his crime-solving abilities were no better than his ability to intimidate confessions out of arrested suspects. But he knew enough to know he would need help. So he, in turn, called his friend Dan Landes and woke him up.

"Señor Dani (which is what don Fernando called Dan), I am so sorry for waking you, but I need your help. I would not have done this except this is an emergency."

Dan struggled to wake up—he had been in a deep, deep sleep—but he sat up in bed and said, "No, it's ok don Fernando, what's wrong?"

"Señor Dani, there has been a murder in La Chorrera, in the gay sauna, a murder of the son of a very rich and powerful family. I need your help. I must go there immediately. Can I pick you up in five minutes?"

Dan had been friends with don Fernando for almost ten years, ever since he retired—or rather, was forced to retire—from the Los Angeles police department. Dan and don Fernando were more than friends. They were partners in several discrete business deals, and Dan knew that don Fernando would not be asking this horrible favor unless it was important

"Okay, yes, okay, don Fernando, but give me ten minutes. I need ten minutes. I'll be outside in ten minutes."

"Gracias mi amigo, I owe you," said don Fernando and hung up.

Dan immediately called a taxi and gave him his address. "I need a taxi pronto—in five minutes," he barked into the phone. Then he woke up Magali, the young prostitute who was sleeping next to him in his bed. She was slow to wake, so he shouted at her, "Get up! Get up! I have an emergency. You have to go now! Get up!"

Meanwhile, don Fernando was calling Jorge Manuel. Jorge Manuel was the police chief of La Chorrera. Even though don Fernando had trained Jorge Manuel and had pulled strings to get him appointed to the job in La Chorrera, he knew that the proper protocol would be to get Jorge Manuel's permission to step into the case. It was not a case of legal jurisdiction—such things do not matter in most parts of the world—but it was a matter of showing respect to another police chief's authority. Jorge Manuel, given his history with don Fernando, was of course quick to give his consent. He too had learned who the parents of the dead man were, and he instantly recognized that he would need all the help he could get as well. Don Fernando asked Jorge Manuel to tell his men not to touch anything in the bathhouse until he and Dan could get there. Jorge

Manuel agreed and told don Fernando he would meet him at the bathhouse.

As don Fernando was hanging up the phone from his call to Jorge Manuel, Dan was pulling Magali out of bed and yelling at her. She was muttering but began to comply. Dan started to get dressed and kept barking at Magali to hurry up. Finally he was able to hustle her out the door to the taxi that was pulling up. He did, however, give her an extra fifty bucks over her regular fee and also paid the taxi driver for her. The cab had just pulled away when don Fernando's car pulled up. Dan got in, and don Fernando took off.

The ride to La Chorrera was normally thirty to forty-five minutes, but there were no cars at this time of night, and don Fernando had his cop lights going. On the way, he explained what little he knew. There was this gay bathhouse in La Chorrera, very old, had been there for many year, never made any problems. He knew of the owner, a man named Luis. Luis had no criminal record, ran a quiet business, was well spoken of by the police chief in La Chorrera. The body was that of Ernesto José Pavones, a poor unfortunate mentally deficient man who was the son of Oscar and María José Pavones, a family whose name went back to the very founding of La Chorrera. The Pavones owned more than half the city, and were extremely powerful. They had five children, four of whom were very successful and also influential in politics. Their second son, Ernesto, was born blind, deaf, and mute, but the family had spent millions to care for him, to train him to get around the city using a white cane, and to communicate with rudimentary gestures. Ernesto lived in an assisted living facility that was near the bathhouse. How Ernesto discovered the bathhouse, no one knew, but he had been going there for years, and his family accepted it as gracefully as they could as simply part of his condition. Other than this one aberration, Ernesto was considered a model patient at the assisted living center.

All that don Fernando knew about the manner of death was that there were marks on Ernesto's neck that indicated he was strangled.

Dan listened quietly. He still could not figure out why don Fernando had called him. Finally, when don Fernando had told him all he knew about the situation, Dan asked, "Okay, so I get that this family is important. But I'm missing something. This is a murder case. My background is in white collar crime—why do you need me?"

"Ah well, Señor Dani, yes, well, I should explain that part..." don Fernando said, and then hesitated.

"Yes?" Dan said, not liking the hesitation. Clearly there was more to the story.

"Well, you see, Señor Dani, the dead man's mother, María José Pavones, is very strong... very opinionated... and she does not trust any of the local officials including the local police. I had to get her approval to get Jorge Manuel appointed, by promising I would help him with any difficult cases. I made the mistake one time at a dinner of telling her that I knew many experts from the U.S. who were... well, that I knew them and they would work for me."

"Uh huh... keep going," said Dan.

"Well, there was wine at this dinner party and I may have exaggerated and told stories about all the crimes you and I solved. I may have claimed that you were an expert and that you were, well, a close friend, a close friend who worked for me... a friend I could call on for favors."

"Worked for you, huh?"

"I am sorry Señor Dani, but when Oscar Pavones called me and told me his wife wanted you to be their outside investigator, I had no choice but to agree."

"She asked for me?... I see, I see," said Dan. "And exactly what kind of expert am I supposed to be?"

"Um... a homicide expert," said don Fernando quietly.

"What!? Jesus Christ! don Fernando, You know I only did white collar crime cases—money laundering, bank fraud, computer crimes, that kind of shit. I'm no homicide expert! The only murder cases I worked on was when I was assigned to go through the victim's bank files!"

Dan exclaimed.

"Well, if we could keep that our little secret, Señor Dani," explained don Fernando. "But if you could act like a homicide expert in front of the other people, I would be grateful. Jorge Manuel is young and he won't know, but he will tell Oscar and María José Pavones everything you say or do. They know you are a gringo so they will expect you to be arrogant and give them orders. Just try and act important. Jorge Manuel will have his evidence technicians there to help you, and they are pretty good. You just need to boss everyone around. Improvise, just act like a homicide expert."

"Act like one? Jesus fucking Christ," Dan said, and just shook his head.

"Are you angry with me?" asked don Fernando in a rare moment of candor.

"Of course, this is stupid!" Dan exclaimed.

"Look, I will be honest, Señor Dani. Oscar and María José Pavones are very powerful. If we don't look good, they will cause Jorge Manuel and me to lose our jobs. Gracias a Dios that I had too much wine that night and told stories about you, because it is the only thing keeping the Pavones' faith in Jorge Manuel and in me. So please, señor Dani, do this favor for me."

Dan gave a little snort, and said, "Fucking shit, don Fernando. Okay, I'll try my best to act like a homicide expert, whatever the fuck that means."

With don Fernando's driving and the lack of traffic, they made it to the bathhouse in fifteen minutes.

Chapter 9: THE BODY

Ernesto's body was still in the bed of the private room. Dan stood just outside of the doorway and looked inside. Behind him stood don Fernando and Jorge Manuel. Behind Jorge Manuel was one of Jorge Manuel's evidence technicians. Next to the technician stood Luis.

"This is going to take a while, fellows," Dan said to the four men. Dan stood there, just looking, first at the door, then at the door frame, and then up and down the hallway. He felt some of his prior police training kick in.

"This is the only room on this side of the building?

"Sí, señor," said Luis.

"Hmmm," said Dan under his breath. He looked closer at the door. It was wooden, covered with old paint. It had no door handles on either side, just the simple hook latch on the inside. When it wasn't latched, it naturally stayed open a few inches.

"The janitor was the one who found the body?" he asked.

"Sí, señor," Luis answered again. "The janitor makes the rounds and checks all the rooms before we close, to make sure no one is still inside."

"Did the janitor know who this man was, who his family was?" Dan asked.

"No, señor, none of us knew who he was."

"But you knew he was blind, deaf, and dumb?" Dan asked.

"Sí, señor."

"How the hell did he get here?"

"I only know he walked in with a white cane, and walked out the same way."

"How long had he been coming here?" Dan asked.

"Oh, he has been coming here regularly for several years," Luis said.

"Several years!" Dan exclaimed. "And no one knew him?"

"Well, we could not exactly ask him, señor."

Dan just shook his head, then asked, "And do

customers sign in when they come here?”

“No, señor, of course not,” Luis answered.

No, of course not, Dan thought to himself. Then he asked aloud: “And the door was latched when the janitor got here?”

“Sí, señor.”

“How did he open it?” Dan asked.

“He has a scraper he carries with him. He can open all the doors to these rooms with it,” Luis answered.

Dan took a pen from his breast pocket and pushed the door closed. It closed against the wooden doorframe at the top, but there was a quarter-inch gap that ran up and down along the vertical part of the doorframe. Dan peered into it. With all the lights on in the place, he could easily see the bed and the body.

“All the doors have this gap,” Luis volunteered.

“Why?” Dan asked.

“So we can see in,” Luis answered.

“Of course,” Dan said. He could see how easy it would be to unhook the latch from the outside with any flat object. But he could also envision how easy it would be to flip the latch closed from the outside, if someone wanted to do such a thing and designed something that had an “L” shape.

“And how many people have been in the room since the janitor found the body?” Dan asked.

Jorge Manuel answered this time. “Five officers arrived on the scene, plus the original officer. They all went inside. And I did, too.”

“And the front desk clerk,” volunteered Luis, “plus two customers who were just checking out when the janitor came yelling up the hall.”

“Jesus Christ,” said Dan, under his breath again. “Who were the two customers?”

There was a pause. The group was getting the sense that Dan was not pleased. “Um, señor, I do not know their names,” Luis said. “After they saw the body, they left, but I know them. They are regulars, good men.”

Dan turned and looked at Luis. “Is there a

surveillance camera at this front counter?" he asked.

"Sí, señor."

"I want to see that video tonight. Jorge Manuel, if you could have your man dust the door for fingerprints, especially on the latch itself and around the door where someone might grab it."

Dan used his pen to open up the door and stepped inside. The other men started to step inside but Dan raised his hand. "Just the technician, please." The evidence technician stepped inside with his large evidence briefcase, clicked it open and pulled out a small aerosol can, a roll of tape, and a camera.

While the technician was spraying the door for prints, Dan was just standing there looking over every inch of the floor. He squatted down and peered under the bed. "Hand me a flashlight," he said to the technician, "and a pair of gloves." The technician reached into the suitcase, and handed Dan a small penlight and a pair of latex gloves. Dan put the gloves on and, shining the flashlight under the bed, reached behind the front bedpost and picked up a small object. He stood up and examined it. It was a small tube of lubricant, mostly squeezed flat, but with a small bead of lube glistening at the open cap.

"Here, dust this," he said to the technician.

The technician sprayed the tube with the aerosol can, and a few black lines of a partial print appeared magically on the metal tube. Dan held the tube steady, as the technician photographed it, and then he placed it in a plastic envelope.

Then Dan turned his attention to Ernesto's body.

"Did your men take photos?" Dan asked Jorge Manuel.

"No, señor. Once don Fernando called, we stepped out of the room and waited."

"Ok," Dan said. Then, turning to the technician, he said, "By the way, what is your name?"

"Javier, señor."

"Ok, Javier, let me use the camera for a bit."

Javier handed him the camera, and Dan proceeded

to take multiple pictures of the body, especially the neck. Then he said to Luis, "So when the janitor found the body, it was against the wall? Is that what you told me earlier?"

"Sí, señor."

"And this janitor, he's still here, right? He's the one sitting in the lobby?"

"Sí, señor."

"Ok, I would like to talk with him when we're done here. He looks pretty old."

"Sí, señor, but he is very smart."

"Okay, okay, so your understanding is that when he tried to wake this guy, the body rolled over as we see him now, on his back?"

"Sí, señor, that is what Tacho told me."

"Who?"

"Tacho, the janitor."

"Oh, ok."

Dan looked at the sheet that covered the body. He took his pen and started to lift some of the folds of the sheet.

"What's this?" He said out loud. "Javier, hand me an envelope." Dan took the clear plastic envelope and scooped up the small amyl nitrate bottle, sealed the envelope, and handed it to Javier.

"It's a popper bottle, Javier. Tell the lab to be careful, not to breathe it, but to check it for fingerprints and DNA, and to analyze the contents."

Dan examined the rest of the sheet and then slowly pulled it completely down, exposing Ernesto's nakedness. He gestured to don Fernando and Jorge Manuel to come in. He took some more pictures and then he said to Jorge Manuel, "Do you see his position—how he's laying on his own hands? Doesn't that strike you as odd?"

"He did not fight back?" Jorge Manuel ventured.

"Right, yet the strangle marks are violent," said Dan. "See how they cover so much of his neck? He was turning his head violently and trying to resist," Dan said as he continued taking pictures.

In actuality, Dan had no idea if the thick marks that

covered most of Ernesto's neck indicated that it had been a violent struggle. Dan had never seen a strangled victim up close in person, but it seemed reasonable and it sounded good, so he continued. "That means he was fighting back, but he couldn't use his hands somehow. And the man who did this was strong—look how deep those impressions are on his neck." Dan turned Ernesto's head to get a few shots of the other side of his neck, and felt the rigidity of his neck and jaw. He then reached down to the ankles and tested their flexibility. Then he lifted the whole lower leg and tried to bend it at the knee. He tried to remember what they had told him decades ago at the police academy.

"Do you see how stiff his neck is?" Dan asked as he moved Ernesto's head left and right, then reached down to Ernesto's feet, and said: "But see here, how his ankles can still move but not his knee so much? Rigor mortis starts anywhere between two and six hours after death, but it starts at the head and moves downward." Dan kept directing his comments to Jorge Manuel, as don Fernando had suggested. "This man has been dead only six to seven hours."

" Javier, do you have a digital thermometer in that kit?"

"Sí, señor."

"Let me have it please." Javier did so, and Dan rolled the body over, exposing Ernesto's naked backside. Dan separated the man's butt cheeks with the fingers of his left hand and inserted the thermometer into Ernesto's anus. He noticed it went in easily. "Javier, there is lubricant in this man's ass. We'll need a sample of that, to see if we can match it to the lubricant in that tube, but also to see if there's any semen inside him."

The thermometer beeped, and Dan removed it and looked at the reading. Then he looked at his watch, and pretended to do a quick calculation in his head, and said to both don Fernando and Jorge Manuel, "This man was murdered at approximately 6:30 p.m. So when we look at the video, let's focus on who left the bathhouse after 6:30 this evening." In reality however, Dan had no idea how to do the temperature/time calculation—it was just something he had read about in a crime journal once. He had made his guess based on the rigor mortis in the neck.

With Ernesto's body lying against the wall, the men could see Ernesto's arms.

"Look at his wrists," Dan said.

The men leaned forward.

"Here," said Dan, "see how they are chaffed right here, and here, where the skin has been rubbed away, and there's still a tiny bit of redness. His hands were tied." Dan started taking pictures, and then stopped, pointed at the locker room key still on Ernesto's wrist, and asked Luis: "What is this, a locker key?"

"Sí, señor."

Dan took a few more close-ups of the wrists, and then handed the camera back to Javier. Then he rolled the body over onto its back again and just looked at it for a minute.

"Ok, I'm almost done here. Javier, would you do a DNA swab on this guy's penis? And take several swabs all around his throat, and one on the inside of his mouth, and as I said, get a good sample of that lubricant in his rectum."

Dan stepped back into the hallway. "Señor Luis, would you do me a favor and go tell the janitor I'd like to talk with him, but reassure him that he is no way in any kind of trouble. I just need his help. And we'll meet you in the lobby in a few minutes."

After Luis walked away, Dan said to don Fernando and Jorge Manuel, "Okay, here's my best guess so far: The two men did not know each other. This was not a lover's quarrel. They were strangers. But it wasn't a robbery. I bet if we check his locker, we'll find his wallet and all his money still there." He turned to Javier and said, "Do me a favor, Javier. Will you make sure we get an inventory of everything in the man's locker? Can you do that tonight?"

"Sí, señor."

Turning back to don Fernando and Jorge Manuel, Dan continued thinking aloud, "So... not a robbery... not a crime of passion... what else do we know? The killer fucked him in the ass, because there was lubricant... The killer somehow gets the guy to put his hands behind his back... what? And then fucks him?... Something goes wrong?... And he has to kill him?... No, because the killer somehow flipped the latch from the outside to hide the crime, which means it was premeditated, because he would have had to have a tool with him to do that... So it's not a case of something going wrong, because it was premeditated, and he picks a victim who can't see or hear or speak... not to mention that he picks the room that happens to be in the most remote corner of the bathhouse. So far it's got all the red flags of serial sex killer, except we've only got one body."

Dan thought for a moment more, then looked at Jorge Manuel and asked, "How many other bathhouses are there in La Chorrera?"

"This is the only one, señor."

"Any other murders like this one?"

"No, señor, none that I've ever heard of."

"Well," don Fernando, interjected, "there have been other deaths here."

"Really?" said Dan.

"Well, yes, that is true," said Jorge Manuel, "but they were all natural causes."

"Like what?" asked Dan.

"You know, overdoses, heart attacks..." said Jorge Manuel.

"Uh huh... natural causes..." said Dan. "Well, let's go talk to the janitor and look at some surveillance videos."

Chapter 10:   BETA

"So you saw this guy leading this blind guy—what was his name? Ernesto? You saw this guy leading Ernesto by the hand into that back room?"

Dan was sitting in the locker room of the bathhouse, talking with Tacho.

"Sí, señor."

"Did you get a good look at this guy?"

"Sí, señor."

"Can you tell me what he looked like?"

"He was not very tall, but very muscular. I have seen this type before—the shorter gay men, they sometimes work out in the gym a lot, you know, to look good, because they cannot look tall. He was not very dark. He had lighter skin, like coffee with a lot of cream, and his hair was short and brown. I thought he was from Argentina."

"Argentina? Really? Why did you think that?" Dan asked.

"It was just an impression, señor... his skin color, his thin nose... if I had heard him talk I would have known for sure... but I never heard him talk... People don't talk much in here."

"Yeah, I guess not," Dan said, and then asked: "And what was the thing you said earlier about him looking like a wolf?"

"Well, his hair... it started low on his forehead. That's one of the reasons I thought he looked like a wolf, because of his hairline. But also because of the eyes. They were always looking, left and right. Even the muscles between his eyes were big because of how he furrowed his brow."

For an old man, Dan thought, an old man who worked in a dark bathhouse, this guy was pretty good.

"Do you think you could draw his face for me?" Dan asked.

"I can try, señor," Tacho said.

Dan got up and went and asked Luis for some paper and a pencil. Luis came back with some lined paper and a pen. "It's all I could find, señor," Luis said.

"That's fine," said Dan and he walked back to Tacho and handed him the paper and pen and said, "Don't worry about how good it is—just see if you can draw his face—how he looked."

"Sí, señor."

Dan was about to let Tacho alone to draw, but then another question occurred to him.

"Tacho, do you know what Amyl Nitrate is?" he asked.

"No, señor."

"Do you know what poppers are?"

"Oh sí, the little bottles that the men sniff."

"Right... do you think Ernesto used those?" Dan asked.

"I do not think so señor. In all the years he came here, I never saw him carry anything in his hands. He needed both hands to find his way around," Tacho said.

"Okay, thanks... go ahead and draw," Dan said. Then Dan went back to front counter where Luis was still standing.

"Luis," Dan said, "I understand this is the only gay bathhouse in La Chorrera, right?"

Luis nodded his head and said, "There is one adult theatre and two or three gay bars, but this is the only bathhouse."

"Where's the next closest bathhouse from here?" Dan asked.

"In this country?"

"Uh huh."

"That would be Umano's in San Felipe. It is a nice place."

"And after that?" Dan asked.

"You would have to go to Grados in Colón, but I do not recommend it."

"Why not?" asked Dan.

"Colón is a dangerous place, and Grados is, well, it's not really a bathhouse. Yes they have a small steam room, but they specialize in dungeons and whips. Men go there who like to beat or be beaten."

"Really?   Hmmm, okay... and outside of this country?" Dan asked

"Well, every country has bathhouses, señor. There are some big ones in Medellin and Bogotá."

"Okay... okay... Do you have the video set up so we can watch it in a bit?"

"Sí, señor, I have them right here," Luis said, holding three black rectangular objects in his hand.

"What are those?" Dan asked, and then recognized them. "Beta? Are those Betamax tapes?"

"Sí, señor, it is an old machine, but it still works."

"Jesus," said Dan, "Okay, well, okay... Does it have a timestamp?

"No, señor, but it shows the clock on the wall above the counter. That's how we know what time it is on the video."

"Okay... okay... well, get it set up, but just give me a few more minutes."

Dan walked back to where Tacho was sitting, hunched over and drawing intently. Dan looked over his shoulder at the drawing and almost gasped. This janitor was fucking good.

"Shit, Tacho! You're an artist! That's amazing," Dan said.

"I like to draw, señor... I am almost done."

"No, no, Tacho, you take your time." Dan walked back to the counter. He could see Luis in the backroom behind the counter adjusting the controls on an old Sony Betamax machine. "Luis," he called out. "Come here a sec."

Luis stepped out of the room.

"Sí, señor?"

"Luis, did you ever see this guy that Tacho said was with Ernesto?"

"I do not think so, señor. I am usually in the back with the books. Tacho described him to me, but he did not sound like anyone I knew. He was not a regular. Maybe when I see the video."

"Okay, okay," Dan said, and then he walked back to Tacho.

"I am finished, señor," said Tacho as he handed Dan the sheet of paper. It was a good drawing of a man with a low forehead, a thin nose, and intense beady eyes.

"Thank you, Tacho. This is very good."

"Mucho gusto, señor."

"Just a few more questions Tacho, then you can go home and get some sleep. I know you must be very tired."

"I am, señor."

"You said this man was a new customer here?"

"Sí, señor."

"How new?"

"This was only the fourth time that I had seen him this month."

"So he came once a week?"

"No, more frequent. The first time I saw him was maybe three weeks ago. I remember because he wore a hat."

"Was it an unusual hat?" interrupted Dan.

"No, it was just a hat, a regular hat, what you gringos call a fedora."

"So why did you notice it?" Dan asked.

Tacho paused and looked at Dan as if he was embarrassed to point out the obvious. "Well, señor, most men don't wear hats here. It is not our custom. That was another reason I thought he might be a foreigner. Argentines love hats. But the main reason I noticed it was because he wore it all the way into the locker room and didn't take it off until he had taken all his clothes off... and then tonight, he put his hat on in the locker room before he even got dressed, even though it was dark outside. I just thought that was odd."

"Wait a minute! You saw him leave tonight?" Dan exclaimed.

"Sí, señor."

"What time was that?

"About 7 o'clock. I was mopping up in here when he left. I was not thinking of poor Ernesto then. I just saw the man leave but didn't really think about it.

"Okay, okay... how long was he here today, do you think?"

"He got here about 3 o'clock I think, 3 or 3:30," Tacho replied.

"Okay, okay... look, can you take a look at just a few minutes of video for me, to see if you can tell me which customer he is? Then you can go home, I promise."

"Sí, señor."

Dan and Tacho walked into the back room behind the counter. There was a small TV monitor next to the BetaMax machine. Luis inserted the first Beta tape into the machine and hit Play. Static flickered across the small screen and then an image appeared. It was a black and white image of the front counter. The camera was set high, giving a bird's eye view of the men coming into the lobby of bathhouse where the counter was. Once the men had paid the entrance fee at the bullet-proof window outside, they were buzzed into the lobby area, where the clerk handed them a towel, sandals, and a lock and key for the locker room, which was off-camera to one side. The clock on the wall in the video said 1:00.

"We start the tape every day at 1:00," Luis explained. "Each tape records for four hours, and then rewinds automatically. So we used three tapes a day. If there are no problems, we record over them the next day."

"I see," said Dan. "Well, let's look at the second tape. That would start about 5:00, right?"

"Sí, señor," Luis said, and ejected the first tape, inserted the second tape, and hit Play. Again there was static, and then the image appeared. The clock on the wall now said 5:05.

"Ok, Luis, keep it in the play mode, but hit fast-forward, and just stop it when someone is checking out."

In the fast-forward mode, white lines moved across the screen but Dan could see the clerk behind the counter whipping back and forth in fast motion, checking in customers, and handing them sandals, a towel, and a lock and key. One thing about Beta, Dan thought to himself, it was always a better picture than VHS, even in the fast-forward mode. The clock on the wall was moving. At 5:20, a man approached the counter from the locker room side of the screen. Luis released the fast-forward button and the tape played in real time.

"Ah, I know him," said Luis. "That is Miguel, a fine man. Owns a good restaurant here in town." Luis hit the fast-forward button again and held it down. At 5:30, another man moved toward the counter to check out. Luis released the fast-forward button.

"I do not know his name, but he comes here often. A very nice man," Luis said.

Luis did not know the man's name, but Dan did. It was his friend Ricardo from Villa Rosario. Dan bit his lip and said nothing. This complicated things. He had met Ricardo maybe seven or eight years ago, when Ricardo had first moved to Villa Rosario. He knew a lot about Ricardo. He knew that Ricardo was bisexual. He also knew that Ricardo had lived briefly with Magali, the prostitute that Dan had kicked out of his bed earlier that evening, but that Ricardo and Magali had broken up years ago. Ricardo had once told Dan how much he cared for Magali, but how the relationship just didn't work. Magali had continued to work for Jenny's, the local brothel, for about a year after their breakup but then had moved away. But she had returned recently and was back working at Jenny's. Dan was pretty sure that Ricardo did not know she was back. He had paid Jenny extra to take Magali home the previous evening. The sex had been great, but now Dan sorely regretted being involved with her.

"Keep fast-forwarding to 7:00," he said to Luis.

Luis complied, and only had to release the fast-forward button one more time, at 6:40, when it showed an older man coming from the direction of the locker room and handing his locker room key to the clerk.

"I know him," said Luis. "He is a regular here; one of the parishioners in our church, a good man. He would not have done this."

"Of course not," said Dan, hiding his sarcasm.

Luis pressed down on the fast-forward button again. At 7:05, a figure appeared from the direction of the locker room—a man wearing a hat—and handed his locker room key to the clerk and walked out the door.

"That's him," said Tacho.

Dan could see the guy was short and muscular, but with the hat on, his face was totally blocked.

"Ok, Luis, back it up just a bit," said Dan.

Luis rewound the tape for a second or two, then hit the Stop button, and waited for Dan to tell him when to hit Play again.

Dan held up Tacho's drawing to Luis and said, "Luis, do you recognize this man?"

Luis squinted at the drawing. "No señor, I cannot say I do. But if Tacho says that is him, then I believe it."

"Luis, let me ask you something," said Dan.

"Sí, señor?"

"The way this camera is set up makes it hard to see customers' faces if they are wearing a hat. Wouldn't you have had a better angle if the camera were on the front wall facing the customers as they walked up to the counter, rather than on the back wall facing the clerk?"

Luis' brow furrowed as he thought about this. Then he said, "But señor, if we did that, we couldn't see the clock and we wouldn't know what time it was."

"Right," Dan said slowly.

Just then Jorge Manuel, don Fernando, and the evidence technician showed up.

"We're all finished in the room," Jorge Manuel said. "We took the locker room key off the body so Javier can inventory the locker. Can we transport the body to the morgue now?"

"Um... did Javier take fingerprints of the dead man's fingers?"

Jorge Manuel nodded yes.

"Okay, yes, then you can release the body," Dan said.

Jorge Manuel handed the locker key to Javier. Then he waved at two policemen standing wearily nearby and told them to bring in the ambulance people.

"Let me show you this," Dan said to Jorge Manuel and don Fernando. Dan nodded to Luis, and Luis hit the Play button. The five men watched as Esteban walked into camera range, handed his locker room key to the clerk, and walked out the door.

"I think that's our man," Dan said.

"But you cannot see his face," said Jorge Manuel.

"He looks like this," Dan said, and handed him the drawing.

While don Fernando and Jorge Manuel were studying the drawing, Dan thought for a minute. Then he said, "Tacho, thank you so much. You can go home now. You've been a tremendous help. Luis has your telephone number so we can get in touch with you, right?"

"Sí, señor"

"Ok, Jorge Manuel, can you have one of your men drive him home?"

Dan looked at his watch. It was now almost 5:00 a.m. It would be dawn in thirty more minutes. "Luis, can you make some coffee? "

While Luis made coffee, Javier reported the inventory of Ernesto's locker: a foldable white cane, shirt, pants, underwear, socks and shoes, a wallet with the equivalent of thirty-seven dollars, a few coins, and keys to a door with tag saying "Santa Maria Health Care." The ambulance attendants brought Ernesto's body out on a stretcher, covered in a white sheet, and took it out the front door to the waiting ambulance.

After Luis brought the men coffee, Jorge Manuel asked don Fernando: "Can Javier go home now?"

"Hmmm, not yet," Dan said. "I'm still thinking." Dan knew that most evidence is lost in the first few hours of an investigation because nobody thinks through what clues might be available.

"Luis," he asked, "do we know what locker the guy with the hat had?"

Luis thought for a second, then said, "No, señor. When someone checks in, we just give them a lock with a key."

"How do you keep track of the keys?" Dan asked.

Luis reached under the counter and brought out a large plastic milk crate full of locks with keys inserted in them. Each lock had a number painted on it in fingernail polish that matched the number painted on the key. Each key had an elastic loop around it so that the customer could wear it on their wrist.

"When someone checks in," Luis explained, "the clerk hands them a lock and key from this box. When they check out, they hand the lock and key back to us. If they lose their lock or key, we charge them 40 balboas."

"So... if I check in and steal someone's lock and key, and use that to check out with, no one would know?" Dan asked.

"Well, that is true, señor, but most people here are honest. The men who come to a bathhouse trust each other," Luis explained.

"Hmmm, okay," Dan said, and then he turned to Javier, Jorge Manuel, and don Fernando and started to explain. "Alright, Javier, you've got a lot of work to do. Jorge Manuel, he may need assistance. We've always got to think about how a case will be presented in a court. No one saw who killed Ernesto, so this case has to be built on good circumstantial evidence. So what would be our best evidence? It's the timeline itself. Tacho sees this guy go into the room with Ernesto around 6:00 p.m." Dan paused for a moment. "But Tacho is pretty old. I don't want him dying before any trial. Jorge Manuel, can you arrange for a video deposition of Tacho? Get him sworn in and ask him to testify about what he saw? I can write out the questions for you."

Jorge Manuel looked confused but nodded his head yes.

Dan wondered if this was something they normally did in this country, but he continued describing the work to be done: "If there's semen in Ernesto's rectum, or DNA from saliva on his penis, that would prove that this guy had sex with him... but still, he could claim that someone else killed him—that he had sex with him, but left him alive, and someone else came into the room and killed him... Javier, it looked like there was a partial print on that tube of lubricant, yes?"

"Sí, señor, but only a few lines," Javier said.

"Okay," Dan continued, "we need to test that

popper bottle. What we're trying to do here, gentlemen, is to think ahead to a trial, to presenting a case to a jury. We have to believe we're going to catch this guy and that he will deny it, and that we have to prove it in court... at least that's how we do it in the states... and thus, we need as tight of a circumstantial case as we can build... Javier, you see this box of locks and keys?"

"Sí."

"Well, one of them may have a fingerprint that matches a print you found in the room, either on the tube or the bottle, or maybe on the door. That means you have to go through every key and lock and take fingerprints off of them, and compare them to what you already have. It won't be the very top keys, because he checked out at 7:00 p.m. and everyone else checked out after him, but the keys may have gotten jumbled up, so you have to test them all." Dan thought for a bit more and then said, "You'll have to keep a record of all the fingerprints, in case it turns out that his guy in the hat is not our guy."

Luis spoke up. "If Tacho says it was him, that's good enough for me."

"But it may not good enough for a jury," Dan said. "We need to have as much evidence as possible that puts him in the room with Ernesto when Ernesto was killed."

Dan handled the box to Javier, and said, "I'm sorry, that's a lot of work." Dan looked at the old BetaMax machine. "Ever seen one of these, Jorge Manuel? It's a Beta machine—they existed before VHS." Dan paused, and looked at how young Jorge Manuel was, then asked: "You've seen VHS machines, right?"

"Those are those old videotape machines?" Jorge Manuel asked.

"Right. Well, these are older."

Dan grabbed the machine and turned it half-way around. He was relieved to see that it had video outputs. "Ok, Jorge Manuel, there are three tapes here. You will need to hook this machine up to either a computer or a DVR machine and make a digital copy. But first, someone needs to sit with Luis and go through all three tapes and ask Luis to identify everyone he knows on these tapes, everyone who went in and out of the bathhouse since it opened yesterday. Can you do that?"

"Sitting and identifying people, yes, we can do that. But making a copy of these tapes will take time. I will have to get help from someone who has a computer shop and equipment."

"Well, we don't need the copies right away, but we do need them eventually." Dan replied. "In the meanwhile, take the machine and the tapes with you tonight and create a chain of custody."

"We will lock it up, señor," Jorge Manuel said.

Dan paused. He didn't want to overstep his role—his fake role—as the expert, but he did know a little about police procedure. So he said: "Well, what I mean, Jorge Manuel, is create a log, a record of who has possession of the tapes from the moment they leave here."

"Well, we will have them, señor. They will be safe with us."

"No, no, I understand that," Dan said. "But when this case goes to trial, I don't want some defense attorney keeping those tapes out of evidence because we didn't have a written record of where the tapes were at all times."

"Oh, they could not do that," Jorge Manuel replied. "If I say we had the tapes, then the courts will not refuse them."

Dan clenched his jaw, but just said, "Well, do me a favor. Just keep a written log of where the tapes are stored, and who has them when they are not being stored, okay?"

"Sí, señor."

Dan tried to refocus his thoughts by thinking aloud. "Now, what else can we do here? What else do we know? This guy is no amateur. This was premeditated. That means he's killed before. So we need to look at any other deaths that have happened in bathhouses." He looked at Luis and then at Jorge Manuel. "How do you track deaths here? I mean, if I want a list of everyone who died in this bathhouse in the last five years, regardless of the cause of death...where would I find that?"

Luis looked at Jorge Manuel and then shrugged his

shoulders. "I would ask Tacho," Luis said.

"We could ask the local funeral homes," volunteered Jorge Manuel.

"And if I wanted the names of all the men who died in the other two bathhouses in this country?" asked Dan.

Jorge Manuel just shook his head. "Señor, death is common here. If someone dies, and it is not murder, then we accept it and move on. We don't keep good records."

Dan looked at don Fernando, who just nodded his head in agreement.

Dan was feeling frustrated. No wonder no one ever gets convicted here, he thought to himself. How can you construct a good criminal case, solve unsolved crimes, without good record keeping? He tried to hide his frustration. "I see," he said. "But still, there are only three bathhouses in this country. I would like to know every death that happened in them in the past five years where there was a popper bottle found with the body. I mean, send someone to talk to the owners, the janitors, the police there, the funeral homes. If we catch this guy... when we catch this guy, if we can put him in other cities at the same time other similar deaths occurred, well, it strengthens our case, and it might solve some unsolved crimes. I guarantee that this guy has killed before."

"We will try, señor," Jorge Manuel said. Dan was not convinced, but he reminded himself that this was not his case. His job was simply to act like an expert, an out-of-town expert, well actually, an out-of-country expert. If this case didn't get solved, it would be on Jorge Manuel's shoulders.

"What else?" he said out loud. "What else?... Shit... the press." He looked up at don Fernando. "I would really like to keep this story out of the press. We don't want our killer to get spooked and leave the country. Is there any way to ask the newspapers to hold off from publishing anything about an investigation?"

Jorge Manuel gave a little laugh. Don Fernando just smiled.

"What's so funny?" Dan asked.

"That will not be a problem, señor. Oscar Pavones

owns both newspapers in town," Jorge Manuel said.

Luis spoke up, "The gay community will know someone died here."

"Tell your clients that the police determined it was a suicide," don Fernando said. "Open for business today as usual."

"But I need my locks and keys!" Luis said.

"You will have time this morning to buy new ones," don Fernando said.

"I think don Fernando is right," Dan said. "If our guy hasn't left town, and he hears that the place is open and that it was just a suicide, he might come back. Jorge Manuel, can you put a plainclothes officer here this week?"

"Inside?" Jorge Manuel asked.

"Of course inside," Dan said.

"Señor, I do not have any gay men on my force," Jorge Manuel said.

"Ha!" Luis snorted.

"Look, Jorge Manuel," Dan said. "He doesn't have to be gay. He can pretend to be a new employee, work the front desk. That way if our guy comes back, you can arrest him."

"The problem is, everyone knows who the cops are in this town," Luis said.

Now Dan was angry. He blurted out, "Then hire a security guard! Borrow a cop from another city! I don't care. Do you want to catch this guy or not?"

"Sí, señor," Jorge Manuel said.

"He has to be cute," Luis said. "Everyone knows we only have cute muchachos working the front counter."

"Also," Dan said, "take Tacho's drawing and send it to the police departments in San Felipe and Colón. See if they recognize this guy. And send someone to the bathhouses in both of those cities... no, wait... no... don't send someone. I think we should go. I mean, we need to be there. If you just send a policeman, the bathhouse owners will just say they don't recognize him. After all, Luis didn't know him. I want to see the layouts there, talk to the front desk clerks. Luis, what time do you think the other two bathhouses open?"

"I think Grados has the same hours as us, but Umano's opens at noon. They get a lot of tourists," Luis said.

"Okay, okay..." Dan looked at his watch. He was tired and he was hungry. "We've done enough here. Don Fernando, I would like to go home, get some food, a few hours of sleep, and change clothes. Then I want to meet at Jorge Manuel's office at 10:45. We can drive to Umano's by noon, talk with them, and then make it to Colón by 1:30 and talk with them. Jorge Manuel, can you make multiple copies of that drawing to take with us? And don't forget to get someone undercover here for this afternoon. And Luis, you need to be here to, to help the undercover guy, got it?"

Both Luis and Jorge Manuel nodded their heads, although it was not with enthusiasm.

"Ok, don Fernando," Dan said. "Let's go."

*   *   *

As soon as he got into the car with don Fernando, Dan let out a stream of curse words. "Jesus fucking Christ, don Fernando, what have you gotten me into? I am in way over my head! I can't believe the fucking bullshit I was saying back there. You have got to get somebody else—a real homicide detective—to take this case!"

"Señor Dani, what are you talking about? You were amazing! You were the perfect gringo expert! Jorge Manuel told me he will say great things about you to Oscar and María José Pavones."

"I don't care about that, don Fernando. There's a case to be solved here. That guy was murdered!" Dan yelled.

"True, but thanks to you, we know what the killer looks like. You sounded so good back there, señor Dani, that even I believed you."

"You don't understand. I was making up half that stuff!"

"Ah, relax, my friend, we all do that. Come on, let's get a bit to eat and I will take you home."

77

Chapter 11: COLÓN

In the meantime, Esteban was already in Colón. He had checked out of his seedy downtown cash-only hotel in La Chorrera and caught the next bus to San Felipe. There he caught another bus to Colón, arriving almost two hours before Tacho discovered Ernesto's body.

Colón was Esteban's home base, and as some of you may have heard, Colón is a city so dysfunctional and lawless that anyone can disappear there. Even the normally positive tour books say: "Stay away from Colón. If you go there you *will* be robbed, or worse." While there was a police department in Colón, it only existed to count bodies. If they got an emergency call from certain neighborhoods, they would just hang up—they weren't going to go there, my friends, not tonight or any other night. In the morning, the police would drive slowly around the perimeter of those neighborhoods and look for where the bodies had been dumped.

The Grados Bathhouse was on the edge of such a neighborhood, just dangerous enough to make the police hesitant, but convenient enough that clients came every night. Grados had one of the most secure parking lots in Colón—a flat dirt lot next door, surrounded by chain link and razor wire, with two guards armed with shotguns. The fee to park there was high, but no one complained. Inside the chain link fence, there was a private entrance to Grados.

Esteban didn't have a car. So he always stayed at one of the many squalid nameless hotels around Grados. These places were either hotels that rented by the hour, a place to bring prostitutes; or they were boarding rooms, a place to do drugs, or crash from drugs, or die... or in Esteban's case, to hide.

He paid cash for his room, paying for two days in advance, got a room key, and went upstairs to find the room. The "room" consisted of a bed and a cold-water sink. The bathroom was down the hall. He stepped inside, locked the door, dropped his knapsack on the floor, sat down on the bed, kicked off his shoes, lit a cigarette, and lay back to review his options.

He had almost really fucked up badly tonight, he thought. Fucking blind cretin! Who would have thought that cretin would have been that strong? Still, he managed to escape without being caught. He should have stayed and fucked that blind pig in the ass. Was he was losing his touch? No, he thought, it was better to be safe and split. Who knows if someone really heard that blind retard grunt? No, he was right in leaving. That had always been the secret to his success: careful planning and conservative choices. Still, he had deviated from that tonight, hadn't he? He had strayed from his method and chosen someone younger. Never again! He had thought that the blindness would make that pig weaker, like that amputee in Puerto Vallarta last year—God, that guy was a good fuck, both limbs waving helplessly in the air while Esteban fucked him so hard, finally cumming deep in his ass just as those limbs fell lifeless and still. Well, live and learn: amputees are still possible choices, but blind deaf-mutes are out.

Esteban finished his cigarette and, on impulse, decided to double check his bathhouse "kit". He sat up, reached down and opened his knapsack and took out his little killing bag, and dumped the contents on the bed. Velcro strap? Check. Wire door-latch tool? Check. Nylon strangulation cord with knots on each end? Check. Esteban wished he could have used that on that blind pig tonight—it would have been much easier. Tubes of lubricant? Check. One, two, three full ones... wait! He had entered the bathhouse that night with four tubes, and used one up... Where was the empty tube? Shit! He must have left that in the private room. Esteban sat straight up and thought. He didn't remember picking up the used tube. He remembered wiping the bottle of Amyl Nitrate clean, but he didn't remember seeing the used tube of lube or wiping it clean. It must still be in the bed or on the floor. A moment of panic struck him, but he quickly thought it through: Those little tubes are so small, it would be impossible to get a fingerprint off of it; and even if they could, those private rooms are littered with scrunched-up used tubes of lube, so no big deal. He was still safe. But still, it was more evidence that he had fucked up tonight. Time to tighten back up, get more disciplined...And never go back to La Chorrera again. That place was bad juju.

Esteban repacked his "kit," placed it back in the knapsack, lit another cigarette, lay back on the bed, and thought: The biggest problem was he hadn't gotten his nut off. He was still horny. The point of sacrificing those pigs was the sex, not the other way around. Thank God he was back in Colón. Back in Colón and only a block from Grados. He would go there tonight. He checked his watch. No, fuck, they would be closing in an hour and a half. That's not enough time. Shit. Well, he would just have to wait until tomorrow. That would be better anyway. He could score some meth tomorrow, get there early and fuck a dozen pussy asses. Fuck them hard.

Esteban finished his cigarette, sat up, reached into his knapsack and found the bottle of Ambien, took two tablets and went to the sink to get some water. He needed to get some sleep in preparation for tomorrow.

*   *   *

At 11:00 the next morning, Esteban was still sleeping. Dan, however, was wide awake and riding in the car with don Fernando back to La Chorrera. Dan had managed to get a few hours of sleep, take a shower, and change clothes, and now he felt much better.

"I'm still missing something, don Fernando, I can feel it in my bones," Dan said.

"Oh Señor Dani, I think you are doing a great job. We have a picture of the murderer, and hopefully we will have fingerprints and DNA soon," don Fernando said.

"Yeah...," said Dan, "hopefully. Is there a police lab in La Chorrera?"

Don Fernando chuckled, "Oh no Señor Dani. Everything must be sent to San Felipe for testing."

"Okay, and how long does that take?" Dan asked.

"Six months, sometimes a year," don Fernando replied.

80

"What! Six months to a year? You're kidding," Dan exclaimed.

"Oh no señor, they are very slow."

"What happens to this guy if we catch him?" Dan asked.

"Oh, we keep him in preventative custody until we have the test results."

"For up to a year!?" Dan asked incredulously.

"Sí, señor."

"What if it's the wrong guy? I mean, what if the lab results show it wasn't him?"

"Well, then we let him go, of course," said don Fernando.

"After a year?"

"Uh huh. If it is the wrong guy, of course, we let him go."

Dan was flabbergasted. "And he doesn't sue you?" he asked.

"Sue us? For what? We proved he was innocent. How could he sue us?" don Fernando answered.

"Okay, okay. Wait a minute," Dan said. "Let's say you have a suspect, and you put him in this preventative custody. Can he make bail?"

Don Fernando laughed, "Of course not. He's in preventative custody. We are preventing him from getting out."

"Well, doesn't he have a right to a speedy trial?"

"A what?" don Fernando asked.

"Fuck, never mind," said Dan, and just shook his head.

There was more traffic in the daytime, but with don Fernando's police lights they still made it to La Chorrera in 20 minutes. When they arrived at the police station, Jorge Manuel was waiting with copies of Tacho's drawing. After some brief chit-chat, all three men climbed into don Fernando's car and they left for San Felipe. During the ride, Jorge Manuel updated Dan on the evidence: the Betamax tapes were safely in a locked closet. Luis had come to the police station and they had fast-forwarded through the tapes and Luis had named every customer he could recognize on the tape. Most of them, however, were simply identified as "a regular". Jorge Manuel, however, could name some of them. It was clear to Dan that watching the tape was an eye-opener to Jorge Manuel—that he had not realized how many of his upstanding fellow citizens frequented the gay bathhouse.

Javier had started going through the process of dusting the locks and keys for prints, but Jorge Manuel had finally sent him home to get some sleep. He had dusted the popper bottle, but found no prints on it. Nonetheless, he packaged it up to send to the lab in San Felipe, along with the DNA swab of Ernesto's penis, and the swab from inside Ernesto's mouth. Javier had also gotten as much of the lubricant out of Ernesto's rectum as he could, using a small suction bulb, and all of these samples were packaged up to send to the lab as well. Jorge Manuel said that Javier thought there might be enough DNA from saliva on Ernesto's penis that the lab could analyze, but that he didn't think there was any semen in the lubricant sample, but the lab would know for sure.

Fingerprints and DNA, Dan thought to himself. That's as much as you can usually get from a crime scene. He had done the best that he could under the circumstances, but still, what did he really have so far? Just a drawing from a janitor in his seventies. He really hoped there would be DNA somewhere on, or in, the body. He hoped they could catch this guy and that he would confess. The last thing he wanted was to be called as a witness at a trial. What a travesty that would be! He would be sliced meat under any cross-examination.

"Let me get this straight, *Detective* Landes, or should I say *ex-detective* Landes? Isn't it true you were fired from the Los Angeles police force after a botched police raid?"

"No sir, that is not true. I took a medical disability retirement after I was shot in a police raid."

"And isn't it true that no one would work with you after that botched raid?"

"There were some problems, yes, sir."

"And isn't it true everyone suspected you of tipping off the criminals in that raid?"

"I was cleared of that false allegation, sir."

"And you were acting as a police officer in this country without any jurisdiction, right?"

"Yes, sir."

"And you were pretending to be a homicide expert, right?"

"Yes, sir."

"And you were giving orders on what evidence should be collected, right?"

"Yes, sir."

"And you aren't a homicide expert, are you?"

"No, sir."

"And in fact, you've never worked a homicide case, except as a backup officer, right?"

"That is correct, sir."

"And you want this jury to accept this evidence in this serious murder case against this poor defendant— evidence illegally and unprofessionally gathered by someone with no training or experience, someone whose last police job was a botched raid—is that what you want?"

"Yes, sir."

It would be a depressing scenario, Dan thought. His only hope was that they find this guy and that he confess. He sat quietly during the hour long ride to San Felipe.

Umano's bathhouse was easy to find. Unlike most bathhouses, it had a big sign in front.

"I see they are not shy," Dan said, pointing at the sign as they got out of the police car.

"Well, look where they are," Jorge Manuel replied.

Dan looked up and down the street. He saw what Jorge Manuel meant. This was San Felipe's version of a red light district: five blocks of porn shops, strip parlors, love motels, massage parlors, and various sex shops. Yet, the street looked surprisingly clean and safe to Dan.

Jorge Manuel explained, "Years ago, when the sex businesses got started here, they were springing up in every neighborhood, and the police got tired of all the crime—they were always running here and there, from this neighborhood to that neighborhood to arrest sex workers for drugs or robbery—so the police and the then-mayor and the city council cut a deal with the business owners: they would rent these five blocks cheap to the business owners, and the business owners could build whatever sex business they wanted here, but only on these five blocks, and they had to police themselves. It is a good set-up. Customers, mostly tourists, feel safe coming here. The businesses make good money, and the crime is very low. If a business gets out of line, the city evicts them. The business owners do a good job of policing the area. If someone tries to rob a tourist, the business owners take care of the robber."

"Really? What happens to him?" Dan asked.

"Oh, he disappears," answered Jorge Manuel.

"I see," was all Dan could think to say.

They walked into the entrance of Umano's. It had the same bullet-proof window in the front that most bathhouses seem to have. Jorge Manuel showed the fellow behind the window his police identification, and they were buzzed into the lobby. The lobby, however, was much different than the bathhouse in La Chorrera—it was not dark and worn; rather, it was well-lit and seemed clean. While the clerk went to get the owner, Dan looked around the lobby. He noticed multiple security cameras, placed on different walls. He peered into the locker room. Even it had security cameras. Dan thought to himself: our man would not come here. A hat would not hide him. We're wasting our time.

And true to his intuition, when the owner came out and greeted Jorge Manuel, and looked at the picture, he did not recognize the man in the drawing. Neither did the clerk. The owner called the janitor and another employee over the intercom and they showed up, but they didn't recognize the person in the drawing, either.

Jorge Manuel thanked him profusely, gave him

a copy of the drawing, and his business card. The owner promised he would call immediately if the man came to his bathhouse. Dan thought to himself: that's simply good business—you don't want someone murdering your clients.

Although Jorge Manuel and don Fernando were making motions to leave, Dan had a remaining question. He sidled up to don Fernando and asked him to ask the owner if they could see how the doors locked on the private room. Don Fernando nodded his head and asked the owner. The owner looked confused.

"We don't have doors on our private rooms here, señor," the owner said.

Dan spoke directly to the owner for the first time. "Really? Why not?"

"Well, we have strict rules prohibiting drugs and alcohol here. Years ago people used to use the private rooms to take drugs. So we removed the doors. We just didn't see the need for them. Plus, we are a safe-sex bathhouse," the owner continued, pointing to a large sign on the wall that read *No Barebacking*. "With the doors gone, we can be sure that everyone is using condoms."

"Really?" Dan said again. "And customers don't mind the lack of privacy?"

The owner shrugged. "They get used to it. We are the safest bathhouse in the country. People will trade privacy for safety."

"Okay, said Doug. "Well, let me ask you this—have there ever been any deaths here?"

"Sí, señor, unfortunately, we have had a few."

"Tell us about them," Dan said.

"One man had a heart attack in the steam room last year. We called an ambulance but he died at the hospital. Another was a fellow who slipped and hit his head and drowned in the hot tub. Unfortunately he was alone, and we found his body later. Then we had one overdose, a German man I think, young man, he had bought some bad drugs and took them before he came here. He died right here in the lobby, right after he checked in."

None of these fit the bill, Dan thought. Then he

asked the owner, "What about that place in Colón, um, Grados? Do you know of any deaths there?"

The owner sighed and said, "Sí señor, there are many deaths there...men get beaten there. It is very sad. We do not allow that thing here. We are a first-class tourist business. They are... they are a place only for degenerates... professional degenerates."

Jorge Manuel thanked the owner profusely again, and the three men left the bathhouse. As they got back into don Fernando's patrol car, Dan was thinking: professional, that would fit this guy... professional *and* sadomasochistic ... that would fit him, too.

"Let's go to Colón," he said to don Fernando.

The drive to Colón took less than an hour, but Dan noticed that both men were unusually quiet during the ride. Finally he asked, "Is there anything wrong?"

"No señor, it is only that Colón is a dangerous place. We must be prepared," Jorge Manuel said.

"Why?" Dan asked, "It's broad daylight and we're police officers.... well, at least you two are. What can happen?"

"Anything," was Jorge Manuel's terse reply.

As they entered Colón, and made their way to Grados, Dan began to get a sense of what Jorge Manuel was apprehensive about. This wasn't so much a city, as a bombed-out war zone. Gang graffiti was on all the walls; abandoned cars, stripped of tires, littered the streets; garbage was piled high everywhere. The further into the city they drove, the worse it got. Dan began to feel very conspicuous being in a marked police car. He could feel the contempt of the people who glanced at them from the sidewalk. Cars of teenagers veered close by, shouting and laughing at them, and sped away. They passed one burning car.

As they approached Grados, Jorge Manuel said to don Fernando, "Since we are driving a marked police car, I think we should park in their parking lot. It'll be expensive, but...."

"No, I agree," said don Fernando.

They drove through the gate of the fenced in dirt lot next to Grados. Two tattooed men, obviously members of some gang, shotguns in hand, approached the car from either side. Dan felt frightened. One of the gangsters bent down to the driver's side and said, "Help you, gentlemen?" in the flattest tone that Dan had ever heard.

"We have a little business inside, maybe ten minutes" said don Fernando. "How much to have you watch our car?"

The man looked at the car. "One hundred balboas."

"I'll give you one hundred now and another hundred when we come out, if no one fucks with the car," don Fernando said.

The man smiled. He was missing his front teeth. "Deal," he said.

Don Fernando parked by the entrance door, and all three men got out. Don Fernando handed the man two fifties, and they walked inside.

"That's extortion!" Dan whispered to don Fernando when they got inside.

"Better that than to lose our car," don Fernando whispered back.

They walked up to the front counter. Unlike the other bathhouses, there was no bulletproof window. They didn't need one. Behind the counter sat three large, muscular, tattooed men. The men were shirtless but each wore a leather bondage top harness with eyelets that crisscrossed their chests. They also wore guns on their belts. One of the men had a sawed-off shotgun sitting across his lap. Dan glanced quickly around the lobby. There were no surveillance cameras anywhere. Over in the corner, a naked young man lay passed out, spread-eagle across a leather couch. Next to him, another naked man was inhaling something from a glass pipe, holding the pipe with one hand and playing with the passed-out man's cock with the other hand. Dan could smell the dirty-socks smell of melting methamphetamine. A young clerk stepped up to the counter, and said, "Can I help you?" Clearly, he knew that they were not customers.

Jorge Manuel showed the clerk his police

identification and said, "May we speak to the owner please?" The clerk looked at the three large men, who nodded yes, and the clerk left to get the owner.

When the owner appeared, Dan thought he had never seen someone so massive. He wasn't so much muscular or fat, as he was just big, a combination of weightlifting and fat. Big, and dangerous-looking.

He looked at Jorge Manuel and don Fernando, and simply said, "Yes?"

"We are looking for this man," Jorge Manuel said, and placed a copy of Tacho's drawing on the counter. "Have you seen him?"

"No," said the man, without looking at the drawing.

"We think he is murdering customers of bathhouses," said Jorge Manuel.

"Never seen him," the man said, still without looking at the drawing.

There was a silent pause, and then don Fernando said, "We also think he is robbing bathhouses and setting them on fire."

The big man's brow furrowed. He looked at don Fernando and said, "No one robs us and lives," but he did look down at the drawing. Then he looked up and said again to Jorge Manuel, "Never seen him."

"Mind if we look around a bit?" Jorge Manuel asked.

"Yes," said the big man, and the three men behind him stood up at once.

"You need to leave now," said the big man.

At this point, Dan completely understood Jorge Manuel's earlier apprehension. They were no match for the four large men in front of them, and certainly no match for a sawed-off shotgun. They could be killed here and their bodies and don Fernando's car simply made to disappear.

There was a very short pause, and then don Fernando simply said, "Thank you for your time, señor." And the three men made their way out the way they had come in.

Outside, don Fernando walked around his police car quickly to make sure it had not been tampered with, and then handed the guard several more bills. The three men got into their car and drove away without talking.

Once they were outside the city, Dan, who was sitting in the back seat of the car, noticed that both don Fernando's and Jorge Manuel's shoulders visibly relax. Dan, however, did not share their relief.

"I'm glad to be out of there," said Jorge Manuel.

"We have to go back," Dan announced.

"What?" Both don Fernando and Jorge Manuel said in unison.

"Well, seeing the inside of that place made me realize something," Dan explained. "Remember, this crime was premeditated, but something went wrong. Something went wrong and he had to kill this guy. That's why the strangle marks are so violent. That means he didn't finish having sex!"

"So?" asked don Fernando.

"Well, last night," Dan continued, "I simply assumed this was the crime of a sexual predator, someone who likes to kill during or after sex. But now, I realize it's more than that. With sexual predators, it's not about the sex or the killing as much as it's about having the sex and the killing follow a certain ritual. And usually, these killers are very methodical. If it goes just as planned, they are satisfied and don't need to kill again for a while. And if their plan fails for some reason, they usually back off carefully and simply wait for another victim. Sexual predators usually don't fuck up! They are cold calculating sociopaths. That's what makes them so hard to catch. But this guy is different—he got frustrated; he got frustrated and he got violent. I couldn't figure that part out until I saw those two boys on the couch at Grados. That place is a meth sex club. I didn't think about meth. Our guy isn't just a sexual predator—he's a sexual predator on meth, which means he will have to have sex again very soon. He didn't get it last night; he wouldn't go to Umano's because that's not safe for him—he can't do S&M there and he can't kill there; so the nearest place would be Grados. He could go there, get meth, and find someone to fuck. And he has to do it soon because he is very frustrated. Meth heads are very impulsive...impulsive and compulsive."

"No, señor, he could not kill anyone at Grados," said

Jorge Manuel. "They would just kill him there."

"Only if he's caught. Or, he might not try and kill someone there, but he could get meth there and he could find someone to abuse there, someone to tie up and abuse...hell, he's probably an alumni from there. We have to go back and get inside."

"That is not possible, señor," said Jorge Manuel. "They know us now. We would not get in. It is too dangerous for the three of us to go back."

"He is right, Señor Dani," said don Fernando, "we cannot go back."

Dan was quiet for a moment, then he said, "Okay, so we need someone who can get inside, someone to just get inside and walk around and tell us whether this guy is inside there or not. We just need a pair of eyes, a spy to go inside. Isn't there someone on your force, someone who would fit in there, someone you we can get to go inside?"

"No, señor," Jorge Manuel said, "I cannot ask that of my men, and besides, no one would volunteer for such a job. They have too much machismo pride."

"You can't order someone to do this assignment?" Dan asked in amazement.

"No señor," Jorge Manuel said adamantly. "I will not do that."

Don Fernando turned around to look at Dan and shook his head no, indicating that Dan should drop the idea.

"Fine," said Dan in disgust. "Then let's go to Villa Rosario."

"To drop you off?" asked Jorge Manuel.

"No, to pickup my friend Ricardo. We *are* going back to Grados today, gentlemen."

Chapter 12: THE PICK-UP

As Dan, don Fernando, and Jorge Manuel were driving to Villa Rosario, they were completely unaware that all the while they had been inside Grados, Esteban had been on the same block, three doors down, inside an unmarked doorway, trying to score some crystal meth. By the time the three men got to Villa Rosario, Esteban had scored four packets of crystal, gone back to his hotel, melted some crystal in his glass pipe, and done several hits. He was ramped up, spun out, and ready to do some hard fucking. He got himself together and headed over to Grados.

Esteban was well known at Grados. He was one of the regulars, a "frequent fucker" as the compañeros at Grados would say, one who could be counted on to give the pussyboys a good beating and a solid fucking. For Grados, like most S&M bathhouses, was basically divided into two different types of clientele: the extreme tops, and the extreme bottoms. The extreme tops, like Esteban, liked to tie people up; gag them; then pull hard on their nipples; twist and slap their cock and balls until tears flowed from the gagged pussyboys' eyes; and then turn them over, or tie them spread-eagle to an iron cross; beat them with whips until their backs and asses were covered with welts; then squeeze a whole tube of lube up their ass and fuck them hard. After cumming, they'd wipe their cum and shit-covered cocks on the gagged pussyboys' faces, spit in their faces, and then walk away. On the other hand, the extreme bottoms, or pussyboys as they were known at Grados, only wanted to be dominated, to be humiliated, tortured, beaten and fucked hard. If they found the right top who fucked them just right, they would cum while being fucked, even though their hands were tied and no one was touching their cocks. If they didn't find the right top, well, they might be tied up for hours, stretched out on a bed or iron cross; and every top who passed by might fuck them for a bit and walk away. There were no safe words at Grados, and a bottom could very easily be tied up for four or five hours, pissing themselves, cramped and unable to move, and end up being fucked by twenty different guys. To most of the extreme bottoms, this was heaven. To some of the unfortunate pussyboys, however, this was perforated rectums, hepatitis, and VIH.

In between the extreme tops and extreme bottoms was a mixture of clientele: some who came only to watch and masturbate; some first-timers who wanted to ratchet up their B&D thrills into S&M; and some "switches"—those who could play either a top or a bottom.

But Esteban was an extreme top. He had learned most of his craft here, especially how to appreciate the extreme pleasure of torture. He would never kill here—he liked the place too much. But he would sometimes spend all day here, when he had enough crystal to last that long, just fucking until the crystal ran out. Even when his cock finally went limp from too much fucking, if he still had crystal left, he would stay, just to beat the pussyboys and shove a large dildo in and out of their asses. He seemed to be compelled to keep going until he was exhausted.

But the killing was different. Those impulses came to him in calmer times, or when he was broke and needed money. He might be clean for three or four weeks, then start planning one of his little "adventures," picking out which bathhouses in which cities he would visit, selecting the bus routes, and making sure his passport was current for crossing borders. The planning was thrilling in and of itself, but of course, it was nothing like the actual act of fucking someone while killing them. That was the best. Then afterwards, when he had obtained enough money, there would be another meth-binge. It was a good life.

And so it was this afternoon, as he checked into Grados. He had scored enough crystal to last till closing time; he was eager to fuck, and moreover, since yesterday's debacle, he needed to fuck. He paid his money, got a locker key, and went to disrobe.

*　　*　　*

92

Meanwhile, Dan directed don Fernando to Ricardo's apartment building, then told both men to wait in the car while he went upstairs to talk with Ricardo. Dan only hoped Ricardo was at home.

And Ricardo was. He had just woken up from a nap when Dan knocked at his door. Because Ricardo rarely got visitors, he looked at the window first to see who it was. He was surprised to see his friend Dan. Dan never came over without calling first. He opened the door.

"Hey Dan, what's up? Come on in."

Dan stepped inside and said, "Ricardo, I, um, I need a big favor."

Ricardo looked at Dan. He had been friends with Dan ever since he had moved to Villa Rosario from the states almost ten years ago, but he had never seen Dan look so intense, so focused... so worried. Was he in some kind of trouble?

"Of course, Dan, what is it?"

"Well, look Ricardo, I need to be blunt."

Ricardo gestured to his little table. "Sit down, and be blunt."

Dan sat down and Ricardo took the other chair, and Dan began: "Look, there's been a murder in La Chorrera, at the bathhouse."

Ricardo tensed up. "When?" he asked.

"Yesterday, after you left."

Ricardo let that sink in, and just said, "Oh."

"Yeah, yeah, Ricardo, I know, I know, you're gay or bi or whatever, I don't care. But here's the deal. Don Fernando has roped me into this case—roped me in, in a big way—and I need your help. We have a drawing of the guy we think did it..."

Dan pulled a copy of Tacho's drawing from his pocket, unfolded it and spread it out in front of Ricardo.

"Ever see this guy at the bathhouse?" Dan asked.

Ricardo studied the drawing. "I don't know... yeah, maybe... maybe. But I can't say for sure."

"Well, here's my problem," Dan said. "I've got a hunch this guy may be at Grados tonight."

"In Colón?" Ricardo interrupted.

"Yeah, you know it?"

"Only by reputation, Dan. It's a rough place."

"I know, don Fernando and I got thrown out of there this afternoon. But that's why I need you... Here's the deal. I want to take you there now, have you pretend to be a customer, go inside, walk around, spend maybe thirty minutes or an hour there, just hang out, and just look around and see if this guy is there. He's short and muscular, and we think this is a pretty good drawing. And if you see him, don't interact or anything, just check out of the place, come outside and tell us. I just want someone to go inside and be a spy for us, that's all. You don't have to do anything there... I mean, anything you don't want to do... I mean... look, I just need someone to go inside and look. The bouncers know what don Fernando and I and Jorge Manuel look like, and we can't go back in. But you could. Can you do this favor for me?"

"Who's Jorge Manuel?" Ricardo asked.

"He's the police chief of La Chorrera, and a friend of don Fernando's."

Ricardo looked at Dan, then at the drawing. Then he said, "Just me? No one else?"

"I don't have anyone else."

"And we'd have to leave now?"

"Uh huh, I just got a hunch this guy might be there. You walk around and check all the rooms and he's not there, you come outside. Simple as that."

"Well... it's not that simple," Ricardo said. "First of all, it's a very rough place. One doesn't just 'hang out' there. Secondly, bathhouses are dark—it's hard to see people and, actually, people don't like to be stared at... what I'm saying is... yeah, I can do it, but I can't guarantee I will be able to tell you what you want to know. Places like that have all kinds of hiding rooms, dungeons, dark rooms... he could be there but I might not be able to find him even if I spent hours looking around."

"But you'll do it?" Dan asked.

"Yeah, I guess. Ok, yeah, I'll do it." Ricardo said, and

then asked, "And where will you be while I'm inside?"

"We'll be parked outside, down the block."

"Okay, okay, look, I just got up from a nap. Can you give me a minute to get organized, and I'll meet you outside?"

"That would be great. Thank you. We're parked right outside," Dan said and stood up and walked out the door.

"Shit fuck," Ricardo said under his breath. But then he thought to himself, well, it might be safe enough. He'd just go in and check it out, maybe sit in their hot tub, if they had a hot tub... Who knows, he might find someone cute, better take some condoms and a lot of lube... shit, who was he kidding? Everything he had ever heard about that place sounded horrible, like it was the worst gay biker bar on earth... but then he thought back to the one gay biker bar he had been to, decades ago, back in the states, and remembered he'd had a good time there... so who knew? But still, all the S&M stuff he had heard about Grados...

He went to his dresser and opened the top drawer and took out several packages of condoms and tubes of lubricant and put them in his pocket. Then he opened the bottle of Cialis and took one. Might as well be prepared, he thought to himself. He kicked off his flip-flops and put on some shoes and went outside to find Dan's car.

*   *   *

Meanwhile, Esteban had found a little pussyboy whom someone else had fucked and left tied to a bed in an open area called the fuck room. The fuck room was a place for public fucking with about ten beds with plastic mattresses, each with tie-down hooks all along the sides. There were also two iron crosses in the corner, and a host of ropes and eyelets attached to the walls or hanging from the ceiling. The little muchacho that Esteban had found was tied up to the bed so well, he couldn't move an inch, and he was strapped to the bed face-up, with his legs pulled up over his head and tied to some wall eyelets. His mouth was held open by a ball gag, and a blindfold covered his eyes. Under his ass, someone had placed a triangular pillow, to push his asshole high in the air. This boy looked freshly fucked. Esteban could see lubricant and cum still oozing from his asshole. Might as well add to the joy juice, Esteban thought, and climbed up onto the bed. He had stroked himself to get hard back in the locker room and then tied a leather cock-strap around his cock and balls. He had also taken another hit of crystal there too. That was one of the things he liked about Grados—he could smoke his pipe openly. He stroked his cock a few times more to get himself hard again, and slapped it against the pussyboy's uncircumcised cock. The muchacho's cock seemed to engorge a bit. Maybe this boy hasn't come yet, Esteban thought to himself. Well, good for me. Esteban squeezed a glob of lube over his erect cock and eased it into the muchacho's asshole. It slid right in, but the ass was good and tight. Esteban propped himself up over the pussyboy, holding his elbows locked, and began fucking him slowly, pulling all the way out and then slowly going all the way deep in, as deep as he could. The pussyboy's cock began to get erect, and its pink head began to appear out from inside the dark hood. Esteban increased the speed of his fucking slowly, adding some force to the final inch, driving his cock as far as it would go inside the boy. The pussyboy's cock was now fully erect. Esteban started going faster, still going all the way in and all the way out of the boy's ass, but harder with each stroke. Then he bent his arms so that he was resting on his elbows, and let his weight fall partially on the boy's torso. Then Esteban lowered his head to the side of the pussyboy's head so that his lips were next to the boy's ear.

"How many times have you been fucked today, muchacho?" he whispered. "How many men have fucked your little pussy ass, huh?"

Esteban was fucking the boy hard now. And now the friction of his own belly against the pussyboy's cock only stimulated the lad. Esteban could feel him try and thrust back against him, in rhythm to his fucking, pressing his cock into Esteban's stomach. He could feel the boy's rapid breathing through his nose and he could hear the tiny wheeze of air as it escaped around the ball gag in the boy's mouth.

"I'm fucking you in your worthless little pussy ass," Esteban whispered. "I wonder if you will cum while I'm fucking you, huh?" Esteban reached up and placed his hand firmly over the boy's gagged mouth and started to squeeze the boy's nostrils with fingers ever so slightly.

"I wonder if you will cum before I cut off all your air, you little fuck slut, huh? Think you can cum before I do that?"

Esteban could feel the boy start to struggle, trying to turn his head, but Esteban kept a tight grip on his face, and a gentle squeeze on his nostrils.

"Yes, I think you should try to cum, my little pussyboy. Try and cum before I kill you."

Esteban's pelvis was moving like a jackhammer now, driving his cock deep into the boy's ass. The bed, which was bolted to the floor, was shaking violently. Esteban squeezed the boy's nostrils a little tighter.

"Better hurry up and cum, you fucking little whore, you fucking pig fucking little pussyboy... better cum before you run out of air..."

The boy was trying hard to turn his head. Esteban loved it. And then, driving his cock deep into the boy's ass, Esteban felt himself reaching climax, and suddenly Esteban felt his belly slide a little on the boy's belly. The boy was cumming. Esteban could feel the boy's ass spasm and tighten around his own cock. And then Esteban came too, thrusting himself as hard as he could against the boy's pelvis and ass. Esteban let out a loud grunt, and then another, and then let himself relax just a bit. He released his grip on the boy's nose and felt the boy suck in air greedily.

"Ah, lucky you," Esteban said, "You get to live another day." Esteban felt pleased because this almost made up for that blind fucking retard last night, and he pulled his cock out of the boy's ass, got up off the bed, stood by the side of the bed near the muchacho's face and wiped his cock on the boy's face, spreading lube and shit and his cum and other men's cum all over the boy's cheeks and nose. Then Esteban started laughing and walked away, looking for more pussyboys to fuck. With all the crystal coursing through his body, he knew he could fuck a lot more tonight and be able to cum several more times. This was going to be a good night.

*   *   *

When Ricardo climbed into don Fernando's car, don Fernando didn't seem to want to make eye contact with him. Ricardo had known don Fernando for many years, mostly as a friend of Dan's. Ricardo hadn't liked don Fernando when they had first met, but over the years through various encounters, they had developed at least a cordial—if formal—relationship: nodding to each other at the grocery store or farmers market, exchanging pleasant conversation if they ended up next to each other at some gathering. Ricardo knew that don Fernando suspected that Ricardo was not strictly hetero, but true to the Latino culture, these things are overlooked if they are not out in the open. But now, all of that goodwill might be gone... now that Dan had recruited him to go into a gay bathhouse, exposing his private preferences to don Fernando and this other cop in the car.

Dan introduced Ricardo to Jorge Manuel as don Fernando started the car up. Ricardo was sitting in the back seat, next to Dan, and Jorge Manuel turned around to shake Ricardo's hand. Well, Ricardo thought, at least this guy is friendly.

Jorge Manuel suggested to don Fernando that they change cars and use an unmarked police car instead of his conspicuous Villa Rosario police car. Don Fernando agreed, and they stopped at the police station and commandeered Villa Rosario's only unmarked car—an old black sedan with tinted windows. As they drove back to Colón, Dan

98

and Jorge Manuel filled Ricardo in on what they knew.

"That blind guy!?" Ricardo exclaimed when he heard about Ernesto. "He was the one who got killed!?"

"Sí, señor," said Jorge Manuel. "Did you know him?"

Such an innocent sounding question, Ricardo realized, simply opened up more of his private life. But at this point, since Dan had outed him as a client in a gay bathhouse—since that was the reason he was going to Colón—there didn't seem much point in being secretive.

"I didn't know him, but I have seen him a few times at the bathhouse. Someone told me he was a regular there," Ricardo said. "A strange figure, he would wander around with his hands waving in front of him so he wouldn't bump into the walls... Shit, that's terrible... he never harmed anyone."

"We think that the killer must have picked him because he was blind and looked incapable of defending himself," Dan said, "but somehow something went wrong and he ended up strangling him."

"So you think this guy's killed before?" Ricardo asked.

"Well, yeah, it all just seems too planned out... There's just too many classic signs of a serial killer," Dan said, "a vulnerable victim who gets isolated from other people, who somehow gets tied up, and the fact that the killer was able to lock the door behind him says to me it was planned. At least, that's how I see it. Usually, there's other bodies with a similar M.O., and that's how we know it's a serial killer, but here..." Dan's voice trailed off. "Well, here, we just don't have good record keeping. We have no idea of how many guys have died in bathhouses, here or in Colombia, Ecuador, or Mexico. All these borders are so porous that a killer could travel around for years, for decades, killing gay men, and if it didn't look like murder, no one would know. And even if it did look like murder, well, you know that few of those ever get solved unless there are eyewitnesses."

"Sí," Jorge Manuel chimed in, "we are very lucky to have a homicide expert like señor Dan helping us."

Ricardo looked at Dan. Dan just averted his eyes. "Yes," Ricardo said to Jorge Manuel, "very lucky..."

"Well," Dan said, "the real lucky break will be if the DNA swabs we took from the body match this guy... which is why we need to catch him fast. Most serial killers travel extensively, crisscrossing the country if they're in the U.S., or going back and forth between countries down here. They know that's what makes them hard to find. You can't connect the dots if you don't know where someone's been, which is another reason we need to find him before he leaves the country. Usually, when there's a botched killing, the killer flees. But sometimes, sexual serial killers are so driven by their need for sex that when they screw up one killing, they have to kill again very soon, to feed their compulsion. Our only hope is that Grados is too close and too tempting for him—that he went there last night or today."

"So..." Ricardo asked, "there's no evidence that he went to Colón...?"

Dan took a breath and pursed his lips. "No." he said, "It's just a hunch, a feeling. I tried to put myself in his shoes. This guy is driven to have sex with someone and then kill them, or kill them while having sex with them. But somehow that got fucked up last night, so he's frustrated. He needs to complete his ritual. He can't go to Umano's because there are no private rooms, so Grados is the next closest bathhouse. Plus, it's the kind of place where if someone died during rough sex, it would be considered an accident, so it seems perfect for him...but it's just a hunch."

Both Ricardo and Dan were quiet for a moment. Ricardo was thinking that yes, it was true that Umano's did not have private rooms. That was why he didn't go there, either. Some acts need privacy, and everyone needs some of those acts every now and then. And Ricardo certainly knew what it felt like to be driven by need. So many times, he had made that bus trip to La Chorrera, to the bathhouse, just because he needed sex... sex with someone... anyone. He had no love in his life, and when there is no love, the need for sex, the need to touch another human being's body... becomes overwhelming.

And Dan was thinking about Ricardo's question about Colón. Ricardo was right—Dan had no evidence that the killer had gone to Colón. He was just acting on his own suppositions... suppositions about serial killers, but suppositions based on what? Stories he had heard? Urban legends about serial killers? TV shows? Dan began to doubt himself again. How had he let himself get drawn into this investigation? They really didn't need him. Any rookie detective could have gotten the description from Tacho, or reviewed the video. That evidence technician Javier would have probably collected the same evidence from the crime scene if Dan hadn't been there... All Dan was doing was acting like a gringo—an arrogant hotshot detective. It was all bullshit. Of course, that was exactly what don Fernando had asked him to do... and that was all fine unless the case collapsed. What if they don't find this guy? Or worse, what if they do find this guy and the DNA or fingerprints don't match him?

Unbeknownst to each other, both Dan and Ricardo each were making small imperceptible negative shakes of their heads, as they each reflected on their own life situations.

Meanwhile, don Fernando drove on towards Colón. He was thinking about how alien gringos all were: always talking, always rushing from place to place, never satisfied with anything, always seeking out new perversions. He felt himself lucky. He was married and had two grown children, good children. And when he felt the need for sex, well, he had a good mistress. And if she was unavailable, there were the prostitutes at Jenny's. That was the normal way for men, he thought. He didn't understand these men who had sex with other men. He had learned to not judge them, because Father Lopez at the Catholic Church had told him that it was a sin to judge, that only God can judge, and so don Fernando accepted that. He did not judge the gays, but he did not understand them

Chapter 13: DROP-OFF

Don Fernando parked the car about two blocks down from Grados. Then the three men looked at Ricardo.

"Oh," said Ricardo, "Ah, so um... where is it?"

"On the next block," said Dan, "where that green sign is. See it?"

"Oh yeah," said Ricardo. "Ok, so I'm just going to go in, look around for a while, and come back and report, right?"

"Basically, yes," said Dan, "but don't rush. Explore the place. We need to know the layout in case we have to send an arrest team in."

"Yeah, okay, well, okay, here goes." And Ricardo got out of the car and walked down the street. He was glad it was only a short walk, because this was definitely not the kind of street he would walk down alone. Trash filled the street; graffiti covered the walls; and the sidewalk smelled of dog shit and human urine. When he crossed the street to the next block, he could see a group of young men halfway up the side street, eyeing him. He sped up his walk until he got to Grados' entrance, then he took a big breath, and stepped inside.

He told himself that the trick would be to look very self-possessed, like he knew what he was doing, like he didn't care, to look almost bored, but non-approachable. He tried to imagine how Al Pacino or Marlon Brando would act this part, walking up to the counter to pay the admission fee, chewing on a toothpick or scratching the side of their face nonchalantly.

When he got to the counter, he realized that he didn't know what the admission fee was. He glanced around for a sign, but saw none. He didn't want to ask because that would give him away as a first-timer. It was bad enough he was a gringo—he didn't want to stand out any more than necessary, so he handed the clerk a twenty and hoped it was enough.

The clerk handed him a fistful of bills back and gestured him over to a stack of towels at the far end of the counter. Ricardo shoved the bills in his pocket and told himself he must remember to count it later so he could get reimbursed for this charade. It was bad enough he had to do this without losing money on the deal. He stepped over to where the towels were. What a seedy place, he thought. There were two big goons behind the counter, both rigged in S&M harnesses and both with guns. The locker room area appeared to be over to the right. The clerk handed him a towel, sandals, and a lock and key. Ricardo took them and, still trying to look nonchalant, wandered over to the locker room. He would need the sandals here, he thought, because he could feel the grit on the floor beneath his shoes.

As he selected a locker, he noticed a morbidly obese, hairy, naked man sitting on a bench in the locker room. The man had what Ricardo would describe as monkey hair—long coarse black hair—that seemed to cover most of his body. Because he was so fat and was sitting leaning forward, his man boobs swung heavy and low. They would have been nice female breasts, Ricardo thought, except that they were covered with the same long hair, even over the nipples. Ricardo had studied Tacho's drawing during the ride here, trying to memorize the face, and this fat man certainly wasn't him, but Ricardo looked at his face anyway. The man must have mistaken Ricardo's look for sexual interest because he suddenly spoke.

"We don't get many gringos here," the fat man said.

"That so?" said Ricardo, turning his back on the man and opening the locker door. He started to take off his shirt.

"Yeah," said the fat man, "usually if a gringo comes here it's because he's a bottom and wants a good hard fucking."

Ricardo folded his shirt and put it in the locker. He kicked off his shoes and put the sandals on the floor and stood on top of the sandals while he unbuckled his belt and began to take off his pants. He didn't reply to the fat man, but the fat man continued. "Yup, when a gringo comes here, he wants someone to bend him over and fuck him hard. So tell me, gringo, are you a bottom?"

Ricardo put his pants and shoes in the locker and slipped off his underwear, still standing on top of the plastic sandals to keep his feet clean, and still keeping his back to the fat man. "No," he said over his shoulder.

"Good," said the fat man, "because that means you can give me a good hard fucking."

Ricardo put his underwear in the locker, wrapped the towel around him, slipped off his socks as he put his feet into the sandals, placed his socks in the locker, closed the locker, and locked it, and slid the key's wrist band around his wrist. Then he turned to face the fat man.

"Thanks, but no," he said.

"Oh come on, said the fat man, "you can throw me just a little fuck. I've got a nice tight asshole." And with that the fat man stood up, turned around, bent over, and grabbing both sides of his immense buttocks, pulled them apart, revealing a hideously huge black hairy anus, and pointed it at Ricardo like he was pointing a gun.

"Go on," the fat man laughed, "give it a try. It's all lubed up. You can even wear a condom if you like—I know you gringos like condoms."

"No thanks," Ricardo said as he walked quickly out of the locker room. He could hear the fat man laughing as he walked away.

Jesus Christ, Ricardo thought to himself, I hope that's not a harbinger of what else is here. He walked down the hall, away from the locker room. And there he came to a flight of stairs going up. He hadn't realized how big Grados was—there were two floors. He decided to start on the first floor, walk around, see where things were located, and then go upstairs and explore the second floor, so he bypassed the stairway and continued walking down the hall.

The first room he came to was the main fuck room. Up ahead, against the wall there appeared to be a young man tied up on a bed, with his legs hoisted and tied above his head. This was, of course, the young man that Esteban had fucked several hours earlier. Across the room, there was an older man strapped naked to an iron cross, standing up, like a human X. He was being whipped by another older man, being whipped hard. Ricardo could see large red welts across his back. With each blow of the whip the man cried out. Ricardo squinted to see more clearly. Neither one of these two men fit Tacho's drawing, but as he stared he saw that there was a large black dildo sticking out of the tied-up man's ass. Every third or fourth whipping, the guy with the whip would reach under the other man's ass and twist the dildo in tighter.

There seemed to be a hallway ahead. Ricardo started walking towards it, a path that took him by the young man who was tied to the bed. As Ricardo passed by the bed, he thought he could hear the boy whimpering behind the ball gag. He looked down at the fellow to see if he fit Tacho's drawing. He didn't, but shit, Ricardo thought, this kid can't be more than nineteen or twenty. Ricardo looked at how tight the ropes were around his wrists and neck—they seemed to be cutting off his circulation; his hands were white. Ricardo leaned down and asked the blindfolded boy, "Are you okay?"

"Uh-uh," the boy grunted behind the ball gag.

"Do you want me to untie you?" Ricardo asked.

"Uh-huh," came the garbled reply.

Ricardo looked around and then began to untie the boy's wrists, first the hand closest to him. It was difficult because the knots were very tight, but Ricardo managed to get the arm free. The boy immediately stretched it out and began to rotate his wrist, to get feeling back into it.

Suddenly a man approached Ricardo and said in a menacing tone, "Why are you untying my slave?"

Ricardo looked at the man. He was short and somewhat muscular, but he wasn't the killer in Tacho's drawing either. His tone was certainly threatening, but Ricardo figured he might be able to take him if he landed the first punch. He paused for a minute and then decided to call the man's bluff.

"I'm going to re-tie him differently so I can fuck him better," Ricardo spit out.

The man looked at Ricardo, who was about four inches taller, then looked at the slave, then said, "Okay, but fuck him good. He's here for everyone to fuck. I want him fucked hard," and then he walked away.

Ricardo started untying the boy's other wrist, and said to the boy, "Is that right, muchacho? That you're here for everyone to fuck? Is that what you want?"

Ricardo reached down and loosened the ball gag, and the boy said, "Sí."

"Well, you still don't need to be tied quite so tight," Ricardo said, and loosened the other hand, but did not untie it. Then he re-tied the first hand but left space under the rope, and walked away.

The hallway Ricardo was walking down seemed to twist and turn, going past a slew of private rooms. Unlike any other bathhouse that Ricardo had been in, the men here seemed to prefer to leave their doors open while they had sex. Evidently, Ricardo thought, the fact that the beating or fucking is a public act must make it more thrilling for either the top or the bottom, or both. Luckily, that also meant Ricardo could look in at each man's face. None of them matched Tacho's drawing. He passed men who were tied up in a variety of ways: bent over, hogtied, suspended, spread-eagled, all while being fingered, or fucked, or fisted, or beaten. He passed several rooms where there was just simple fucking going on, or two men engaged in sixty-nine, or rimming. Occasionally Ricardo would step inside to get a better look at faces, and to watch the sex for a bit. While Ricardo was not an exhibitionist himself, he always did enjoy watching people having sex—at least when it wasn't too extreme, when the people he was watching seemed to enjoy it, and especially when the cocks were big and fun to watch. That was one of the appeals of bathhouses—it was simply possible to watch other people have sex without any embarrassment or obligation. To Ricardo, two or more people having sex together was a beautiful thing to watch... usually... but not here. The scenes here were mostly too violent for Ricardo's liking. He came to one large room that had a man sitting on a low stool, shackled to the wall by iron bands around his neck and wrists, while a group of men lined up to fuck him in the mouth. There was a leather pad attached to the wall behind the man's head, and Ricardo soon saw why. There were five men standing in line all watching while the first in line was fucking the shackled man's face. It wasn't that the shackled man was giving a blow job—no, it was all he could do to hold his head against the leather pad while the first man in line fucked his mouth. This must have been going on for a while, because cum was oozing down the shackled man's chin and had already covered his chest. Ricardo walked on. He came to a smaller fuck room with only two beds. Here, a group of four men were holding another man down while a fifth man was raping his ass. Ricardo couldn't tell whether he was watching a scene that the victim had asked to enact—had orchestrated—or whether he was watching a real rape. He hoped it wasn't the latter. While he was fairly strong and knew a little about self-defense, he wouldn't be a match for four men. He looked quickly at each man's face to make sure it wasn't the guy, and then he walked on quickly.

He came to the door of the steam room, and opened it and peeked inside. It was dark and steamy, as it should be. That pleased him, but he decided not to go in quite yet. He still wanted to get more familiar with how the place was laid out first. He told himself he would loop around a bit more, check out the upstairs, and then go back to the steam room and just hide out there until enough time had passed so he could report back to Dan.

The twisting corridor seemed to curve back around to where it started. Ricardo could see the first fuck room just ahead. But just before he got there, there was a sling room—a room with no bed, but just a large hammock-like sling hanging from the ceiling about three and a half feet from the floor. In the sling a rather attractive man was lying, face-up, with his feet propped up in the air resting in special leather loops. The man was naked, not tied up in any way, simply waiting for someone to come in and fuck him. The sling was constructed so that it would hold a man, support his head, back torso, and legs, but the material of the sling was cut away like a "V" so that someone could walk in between the man's legs, stand there and fuck the man easily while moving the sling back and forth in space. The man's cock was half-erect, lying on its side. It was an attractive cock. Ricardo stepped into the room. The man smiled and said: "Just get here?"

Ricardo smiled back and reached over and started playing with the man's cock. As stated, it was a very attractive cock and it was responsive to Ricardo's touch.

"Would you like to fuck me?" the man asked politely.

"I might," said Ricardo, "I just might."

Ricardo was not usually a top, but, as said, this was an attractive man, and even though the various scenes of debauchery that Ricardo had witnessed during his stroll around Grados did not appeal to him, they were not without their prurient effect on him.

"Hang on a minute while I go get a condom," Ricardo said.

"I'll be right here," the man said and smiled.

Ricardo started walking back to the locker room to get a condom and some lubricant.

*   *   *

Meanwhile, Esteban had come to a startling realization. He had just finished fucking someone tied standing up to an iron cross in a fuck room on the second floor. It was difficult to fuck this guy standing up, so Esteban had pulled out, found a whip and began to beat the guy. But he grew tired of that.

"What I need," Esteban said to himself, "is another hit of crystal." So he dropped the whip and headed back down to the locker room. There, he opened his locker, took out his pipe and grabbed the small packet of crystal. But he had smoked the last chunk of meth from that packet when he had arrived at Grados. No matter, he told himself, he had bought three more packets. But when he searched his pockets, he realized that he had left the other three packets of crystal back at the hotel.

"Fuck, shit, goddamn fucking shit," he said out loud. Now he would have to get dressed and walk back to his hotel. How could he have been so stupid? He knew why—he had been spun out when he left the apartment—he had simply forgot to put the other three packets in his pocket. They were still sitting there on his bed.

Luckily for Esteban, Grados had a liberal in-out policy. The management recognized that people often needed to go out and score more drugs, so once a customer paid his entrance fee, he could leave and come back as much as he wanted until closing time.

Esteban was just standing there naked in front of his locker contemplating having to walk back to his hotel, when Ricardo walked back into the locker room to get his condoms.

Chapter 14: SERENDIPITY OF SORTS

Ricardo was thinking about the attractive man in the sling as he went back into the locker room and walked up to his locker. He saw that there was a short muscular man standing two lockers away from him, staring into his hands, but he simply didn't connect that image with anything. He just wanted to get his condoms and lube and get back to the man in the sling before someone else did.

"God dammit to hell," he heard the man say. "Fuck, shit."

Automatically... without thinking about it... the words "What's wrong?" came out of Ricardo's mouth. He had no idea why he said them. It was just his nature to respond to other people who seemed to be in distress. He didn't really want to know what the man's problem was. What he wanted to do was use his key to open his locker and then get his pants, and then reach into the pockets, and grab a condom and a tube of lube. His key was almost into his lock, and as he inserted the key, and turned it, and as the lock popped open, because he had uttered those words, his head naturally turned towards the man to whom he had asked that simple question.

And Esteban wasn't looking at Ricardo either. He was still staring at his empty hands but he automatically responded to the question without thinking and said, "I left my fucking crystal back in the hotel. Now I have to go back and get it," as he instinctively turned towards the person who had asked him the question, just as Ricardo was opening his locker and was turning to look at him.

One of the skills that Ricardo had mastered years ago, years before he had left the states, during those decades that he had worked as an attorney, was the ability to maintain an absolutely deadpan expression. It was a skill one needed in court, where one never really knew what a witness was going to say, but only knew that the most important thing in the world was to never look surprised in the eyes of a jury, to always look in control. And so it was at that moment that those facial memory muscles kicked in, the moment when Ricardo looked at the man standing three feet away and realized that this was the man in Tacho's drawing. And even though Ricardo's face remained totally impassive, a million thoughts raced through his head at that exact moment, such as the fact that he might be standing next to a serial killer in a seedy dangerous S&M bathhouse while Dan was two blocks away; the fact that he absolutely had to not react to this man; the fact that he was going to have to do something now, although he didn't know what to say; the fact that he did know that he was not going to be able to walk back and fuck that attractive man in the sling; the fact that he had about a microsecond to decide whether to simply say "that sucks" and simply get dressed and go out to don Fernando's car even though he knew this man had just told him that he was going to get dressed and walk out too; and most importantly, the fact that for some reason, he was suddenly and inexplicably not wanting to let this man get away. And somehow, from some part of his mind he couldn't reach, he heard himself say, "Really? I was just going to go out to my car and slam some crystal. Wanna come with?" And with that, Ricardo turned his head back towards his locker and reached in and grabbed his underwear and started to put it on, and then added, without looking at Esteban, "It's pretty good stuff."

Esteban watched Ricardo step into his underwear. Ricardo had a nice looking ass. "Yeah?" he said, "you coming back here afterwards?"

"Uh huh," Ricardo grunted and adjusted his cock and balls in his underwear.

Esteban took a short step closer and reached over and felt Ricardo's ass and said, "You coming back here to get fucked? You wanna get high and let me fuck you?"

Ricardo still kept himself from looking at Esteban, but said, "That would be the plan."

Esteban pressed his fingers in between Ricardo's buttocks and pushed the cloth of Ricardo's underwear against his asshole. It sent creepy shivers up Ricardo's spine, but he continued reaching into his locker and taking out his pants.

"Come on, get dressed," Ricardo said, "I need a hit."

"I'll wait for you here, man. Bring the crystal here and we'll get high," Esteban said.

"No," Ricardo said, "my crank always gets stolen here. I keep it in the car. If you want some, you come with me. If you don't want any, fine."

Esteban reached over with his other hand and rubbed Ricardo's cock through his underwear. He wanted to fuck this guy, he wanted to fuck this guy and twist his arrogant cock till he screamed. But moreover, he wanted a hit of crystal first. Ricardo pulled his pants out of his locker, stepped into them, and pulled them up, which forced Esteban hands off his ass and off his cock.

"If you're coming, get dressed," Ricardo said, "because I'm leaving now."

"Where are you parked?" Esteban asked.

"Next block south."

Esteban thought about this. Maybe they could do a hit in this guy's car, and then he could take him back to his hotel and tie him up there. No, that would be a bad plan. Maybe do some crystal in his car, hit him over the head, and steal his crystal. Or maybe just do the crystal and come back here and fuck him hard. Any way he thought about it, he could make it work.

"Okay, man," Esteban said, and started getting dressed.

In the months to come, Ricardo would look back on that exchange, analyze it from every different angle, and still never be able to come up with a rational answer for why he did what he did, for why he said those words; from whence the idea sprang to lure Esteban out to don Fernando's car; for why he took that horrific chance to leave the bathhouse and walk that block and a half with a serial killer, someone who could have easily pushed him down that side street between Grados and don Fernando's car and knifed him. He simply never knew how it was that things unfolded the way they did that night, and could only conclude that it had nothing to do with him at all, but was simply a piece of police serendipity.

Because it all seemed like a dream. He did walk out of the bathhouse with Esteban that night, after they told the clerk they'd be right back, and they did walk the block and a half to don Fernando's car, and the only thing that Ricardo later remembered Esteban saying to him was some question about how much crystal he had, and Ricardo simply answering "enough."

It wasn't until they actually got to the car that Ricardo realized that he didn't know what was going to happen next. The street was dark and don Fernando's unmarked car had tinted windows all around, so it did not appear that there was anyone inside the car. And Ricardo and Esteban walked up to the car just like Ricardo imagined they would, but then when they got to the car, Ricardo simply stopped, because he didn't know what else to do. If it had actually been his car, he would have been reaching into his pocket for the keys, but it wasn't his car, so he just stood there. And in that microsecond, Esteban turned to him and started to open his mouth. Ricardo always imagined later that Esteban was about to say "So what's the problem, man?" or "Aren't you going to open it?" or something, but at that exact moment, the dreamlike quality of the experience ended, and three of the car's doors exploded open with a bang and don Fernando and Jorge Manuel jumped out of the front seats with their guns drawn and Dan jumped out of the back seat. Jorge Manuel got to Esteban first, jammed his gun into Esteban's stomach, put a hand on the top of his head and pulled him face down to the sidewalk. Don Fernando landed on Esteban's back with one knee and held a gun to his head while Jorge Manuel pulled Esteban's hands behind his back and handcuffed him. Dan had pulled Ricardo hard over to one side, out of the way. Both don Fernando and Jorge Manuel were yelling at Esteban, but it all was happening so fast that Ricardo couldn't make sense out of what they were yelling.

Then time seemed to snap back to normal, or near normal, and Ricardo suddenly felt adrenaline hit his arms and legs and he started shaking. Dan held him up and kept him from falling down. Don Fernando and Jorge Manuel were still yelling something at Esteban and started patting him down. The only thing Ricardo heard was Dan shouting, "Good job Ricardo!" into Ricardo's ear.

Then don Fernando and Jorge Manuel yanked Esteban to his feet by his arms and held them there, and all four men just looked at him. Esteban was bleeding from his forehead where he had hit the curb. He seemed dazed and injured.

Dan looked at him and said, "That's him."

And Jorge Manuel looked around and said to don Fernando, "We need to go, now!"

"Sí," replied don Fernando and they dragged Esteban around to the back of the car. Pop the trunk!" don Fernando yelled at Dan.

Dan let Ricardo go and ran to the back of the car and popped the truck. Ricardo tried to maintain his balance but ended up stepping over to the car and leaning on it for support. He looked over at the back of the car. Don Fernando and Jorge Manuel were stuffing Esteban into the trunk of the car. Dan was standing behind them, looking confused. Esteban was starting to regain his wits and started to struggle. Don Fernando pulled his fist back and struck Esteban hard in the ribs. Ricardo could hear the crack of the blow and heard Esteban cry out. They got him in the trunk and slammed the lid.

"Get in, get in!" Jorge Manuel yelled at Ricardo. Ricardo opened the backseat door and climbed in. He felt Dan's hand pushing him in from behind as Dan climbed in after him.

Don Fernando and Jorge Manuel ran to the front of the car and got in. "Go! Go! Go!" Jorge Manuel shouted to don Fernando. Ricardo looked out the window and saw the reason for their concern. Four large men had run out of Grados and were lumbering towards them. They seemed to be carrying rifles or guns. Don Fernando started the car, hit the gas and did a sharp turn down the side street and sped away. Ricardo thought he heard gunfire behind them.

As they sped down the streets and headed out of town, Ricardo realized that all four of them were breathing very hard. He could hear Esteban kicking the inside wall of the truck and shouting obscenities from the trunk. Ricardo looked at Dan. He wanted to ask him what the hell was going on, but he was too winded.

It took everyone about five minutes to catch their breath. Finally don Fernando broke the silence. "Don Ricardo," he said, addressing him with the Spanish appellation of respect, "you did an excellent service for us tonight. I am in your debt, señor." Ricardo had never heard don Fernando speak to him so respectfully. Jorge Manuel turned around from the front seat and nodded. "Sí, both of you gringos have been amazing."

"Uh... why did you put him in the trunk?," Dan asked.

"Well, Señor Dani," said don Fernando, "this is not a big car. You two would not have been comfortable with three people in the back seat," and then both he and Jorge Manuel chuckled.

"You could have called the Colón police to take him into custody," Dan said.

Don Fernando and Jorge Manuel laughed louder at this. "No señor," Jorge Manuel said, "they would not have come. Besides this is our problem, not theirs. We will take him back to La Chorrera where he belongs."

"As if we could have waited any longer," don Fernando added. "I think those men recognized us."

Dan's brow furrowed. "Wait a minute," he said. "How did you two even have jurisdiction to arrest him? How do you have jurisdiction to transport him to La Chorrera?"

"We don't," replied Jorge Manuel simply. "That's why it is better he is in the trunk."

Dan sat the rest of the drive in silence. He didn't mind helping any police department, in what little help he could give... after all, he had been a police officer once too. But here he was helping them break the law. Helping them, hell! He had created the crime! It had been his idea to go to Colón; his idea to do surveillance on Grados; his idea to send Ricardo in; he had orchestrated an illegal arrest and kidnapping! That was the last straw. As soon as this guy was in custody in La Chorrera, he was off the case, done, finished. Don Fernando was on his own now. Fuck... still, he had to acknowledge that this was not the states... that there was a primitive style of justice here, illegal perhaps, but still justice... if they hadn't done what they did, this guy would not have been caught. The Colón police weren't going to do it, that's for sure... this guy, if he was the killer, would have killed again, would have been free to cycle through a half-dozen countries, killing and killing and getting away with it. At least once they get him back to La Chorrera, and get him arraigned, then real justice can take its course. When they get the lab results back, they can have a trial, and then a jury can decide whether or not he is guilty. Dan had done his job the best he could under the circumstances.

Dan stared out the window and thought about these things. Ricardo, in the meanwhile, was filling Jorge Manuel and don Fernando in on how he had tricked Esteban into coming out to the car. Jorge Manuel was thumbing through Esteban's wallet, which he had removed from Esteban's back pocket. Don Fernando was driving and feeling very pleased with himself, very pleased with a good day's work done. They had investigated a crime, and they had a man in the trunk. It had been a good day.

Chapter 15: JUSTICE

After they arrived in La Chorrera and don Fernando stopped the car in front of the police station... and after don Fernando and Jorge Manuel dragged the screaming and kicking Esteban out of the car trunk and hauled him inside the station and locked him in a cell... and after Jorge Manuel came back outside and shook Ricardo's hand and Dan's hand vigorously and thanked them over and over again for helping to capture Esteban... and after don Fernando drove Dan and Ricardo back to Villa Rosario... and after don Fernando dropped Ricardo off at his apartment and again offered his personal thanks to Ricardo... and after don Fernando dropped Dan off in front of his apartment (thanking him as well)... and after Dan watched don Fernando drive off into the night... Dan turned and walked the four steps up to his gated apartment building, let himself inside, went up to his apartment, unlocked the door, went inside, and headed straight for the refrigerator. He pulled out a bottle of guaro from the freezer and poured a glassful over ice and sat down at his dining table and drank it down quickly. He could feel the freezing liquor make its way down into his stomach and it felt good. He got up and poured another and sat back down to think. His mind was still turning over all the loose ends and problems with this case, still trying to come to some resolution he could live with. He tried to focus on the positives: If don Fernando's job (and Jorge Manuel's job as well) had actually been in jeopardy because of whatever don Fernando had stupidly promised this Pavones family, well at least Esteban's capture protected those jobs... and don Fernando was, after all, his friend... so their jobs were safe, assuming the lab results came back and connected this guy Esteban with the dead man... and if, those lab results took six months or more to come back like don Fernando had said, well, that would allow Jorge Manuel to keep the investigation open and look at any other leads...

Dan took another sip of his drink. The problem was, Dan knew how the police system worked down here.

Probably, in Jorge Manuel's mind, the investigation was closed. He wouldn't keep looking for any other suspects. Dan made a mental note to encourage don Fernando to tell Jorge Manuel to keep investigating the case. But still, it was no longer Dan's problem. He had done what don Fernando had asked him to do. He was off the hook. And in fact, don Fernando owed him a huge debt. Dan wondered how he could parlay that debt into something tangible. But then his mind came back to Ricardo, because Dan, in turn, owed Ricardo a huge debt. If Ricardo had not lured that guy out to the car, probably they never would have captured him. If Ricardo had simply come back to the car saying he hadn't seen Esteban inside Grados, Dan didn't know what he would have done as a next step: keep sending Ricardo in day after day? What a fucking stroke of luck that things had turned out this way, despite the illegality of it all. He took another sip of guaro. Yes, he had been lucky, extremely lucky. Somehow he had come out of this stinking mess smelling like a rose... all due to luck. What a crock of shit... what a crock of lucky shit.

He finished his drink and realized how exhausted he was. He lay down on the bed, still in his clothes, and quickly fell asleep.

*   *   *

And Dan was still asleep the next morning at 9 a.m. when his phone rang. When he first opened his eyes, he didn't know where he was; then he realized he was lying in his own bed; but he couldn't remember how he got there; but the phone kept ringing; and then Dan remembered; and so he got up and answered the phone. It was don Fernando.

"Ah good morning, señor Dani," don Fernando said, sounding very chipper. "I hope I am not interrupting your breakfast."

"No, no," Dan said. "in fact, I was still in bed."

"Ah, forgive me, yes, you probably were very tired. I am sorry to wake you, but I have good news."

Dan rubbed his eyes. "Yeah?" he said. "Tell me."

"Oscar and María José Pavones want to meet you.

118

They want to personally thank you."

"Yeah?" said Dan, "Is that the good news?"

"Sí, señor Dani, it is quite an honor. I will pick you up in thirty minutes and we will drive to La Chorrera."

"What?! No, no don Fernando, is this necessary? I mean, really... you go. I don't need to be there."

"Oh no, señor Dani, they asked for you. You must come!" said don Fernando. "They are very important people and to refuse a request to be thanked by them would be an insult."

"Oh, fuck, shit," Dan said. "Okay, but I need to shower."

"Yes," said don Fernando, "I will pick you up in 30 minutes. And wear a tie."

*   *   *

Don Fernando was waiting in his car when Dan stepped out of his apartment building forty minutes later. The delay had come because Dan had to search high and low to find a necktie. It had been years since he had worn one, but finally he found one in the side pocket of an old suitcase.

Don Fernando turned his police lights on and drove like crazy, weaving through traffic. "We cannot be late," he explained.

"Why not?" Dan asked, "Aren't we on Latino time?"

"No, not with the Pavones. This is very unusual event, señor Dani. Oscar and María José Pavones rarely leave their compound. For them to come to the police station is a very important occasion, not only for you and me, but for Jorge Manuel. He will have a job for life now."

"Hmmmpf," muttered Dan. "Good for him."

"And I think they will have a gift for you, señor Dani," don Fernando added slyly.

"Really?" ask Dan, "What kind of gift?"

"I do not know. All Jorge Manuel told me was that Oscar Pavones told him there was going to be a presentation."

"I hope it's money," Dan said, and looked out of the window. But then he turned to don Fernando and said, "What about Ricardo? Does he get a gift too?"

"Oh, no," said don Fernando. "We did not tell the Pavones about Ricardo."

"Why not?" asked Dan.

"Well... why complicate the story? The Pavones believe it was our superior police abilities," replied don Fernando.

"Right..." said Dan. "Why complicate it?" and he sunk back in his seat.

*   *   *

As soon as Dan stepped inside the police station in La Chorrera, he could tell it had been freshly scrubbed and mopped inside—it still smelled of bleach. All the desks had been cleaned and all loose papers removed from the desktops and probably stuffed inside drawers. A row of police officers in uniform stood at attention against the wall. There was an air of official tension about the place. In the middle of the room stood Jorge Manuel, also in full uniform, and an older couple, both dressed in black. Even from across the room, Dan could tell the man's suit was expensive. The woman wore a black veil over her face. They seemed to be chatting seriously with Jorge Manuel, whose brow was furrowed but was nodding in agreement with them. As don Fernando and Dan walked in, Jorge Manuel gave a little smile, and said something to the couple, and the couple turned towards them.

Dan was trying to follow don Fernando's lead as they walked across the room. Jorge Manuel greeted don Fernando and introduced Oscar and María José Pavones to Dan. The men all seemed to be shaking hands. Dan held back a bit until María José Pavones came up to him, took his hand in hers, and lifted her veil. Dan could see that her eyes were puffy, even through the heavy make-up, and that she had been crying. She leaned forward, gave him a kiss on the cheek, and said in a low hoarse whisper, "I just want to thank you for helping to capture our son's killer," and then she kissed his cheek again.

Dan didn't know what to say. He hadn't expected to be confronted with the family's suffering, so he just said: "Anything for you, señora." Evidently, that was the right thing to say, because she smiled, and then lowered her veil and stepped back to her husband's side.

Then Oscar Pavones spoke to Dan. "Officer Landes, on behalf of the entire Pavones family, our parents and grandparents in heaven, our children and our grandchildren, to express our deep gratitude, we would like to present you with this gift." He held out a large book with a gold embossed cover that read *The History of the Pavones Family* above an official picture of Oscar and María José Pavones sitting formally, surrounded by fifteen or twenty family members of all ages. Dan could see don Fernando nodding to him. Dan stepped forward, accepted the heavy book with both hands, bowed and said, "This is a great honor, señor. Thank you," and stepped back. The book was massive and heavy. Oscar Pavones then nodded to Jorge Manuel, who stepped forward and whispered something to don Fernando. Dan could see don Fernando's eyes widen in surprise, his brow furrow, but then he nodded, and whispered something back to Jorge Manuel. Jorge Manuel then turned to the group of police along the wall, and announced, "Dismissed" in a curt tone. The policemen who were lined up against the wall all filed out of the building, all except for one sergeant who remained.

When the policemen were all gone, Jorge Manuel said to Dan, "The Pavones want to see their son's killer." Dan looked at Jorge Manuel, opened his mouth, and was about to say that this was a horrible idea when he saw don Fernando gesture to him to keep quiet. Dan closed his mouth and said nothing. Jorge Manuel turned and led the group through the door that led to the police station's lock-up cells. Jorge Manuel led the way followed by Oscar Pavones, and then María José Pavones, then don Fernando, followed by Dan. They passed through several sally ports, finally arriving at a room that held three cells, three 10x10 areas created by steel bars that ran floor to ceiling. The first and third cell was empty. Esteban was in the middle cell, sitting on a thin mattress atop a steel bed attached to the wall. He looked horrible, and Dan wondered if he was going through some type of withdrawal or whether he had been roughed up. He seemed to have a lot of bruising around his head. Maybe from being banged around in the trunk, Dan thought. His hands were behind his back. As the five people approached the cell, Esteban jumped off the bed and started yelling at them.

"Do you think you can take these cuffs off me?" he shouted. "How can I sleep with cuffs? How can I drink water? How about some food too?! And I want to call a lawyer. Take these cuffs off me!"

"Yes," Jorge Manuel shouted, "We will do that in a minute, for sure."

"Who are these people?" Esteban shouted, looking at Oscar and María José Pavones.

"The parents of the boy you killed," don Fernando said softly. Esteban looked at don Fernando, then he turned his head and stared at Oscar and María José Pavones for a moment... and then he just smiled. Dan thought it was the most evil smile he had ever seen. Don Fernando nodded to Jorge Manuel, and Jorge Manuel took his service pistol out of his holster and held it out to Oscar Pavones. Oscar Pavones took it and without saying a word handed it to María José Pavones.

What happened next seemed to unfold in some alternate universe—a slow motion film that Dan was unable to stop. María José Pavones raised the pistol and aimed it at Esteban's chest. Esteban's eyes widened but he had no time to react. María José Pavones pulled the trigger, there was a loud explosion, and Esteban's chest caved in from the bullet, and he cried out and stumbled backwards against the steel bed, his head flying forward. Dan dropped the book he was holding and started to raise his arms toward María José Pavones to grab the gun, but don Fernando swung his arm hard across Dan's chest, stopping him from moving forward, and then grabbed

Dan's arm. Blood was gushing from Esteban's chest. He looked up at María José Pavones. It was a look of complete terror. Then María José Pavones handed the gun to Oscar Pavones, and Oscar Pavones aimed the gun at Esteban's face and pulled the trigger, and the right side of Esteban's head exploded off and splattered against the wall, and the rest of Esteban's body fell to the floor. Blood poured out of the side of his head where that half of his skull had been. Oscar Pavones handed the pistol back to Jorge Manuel who put it back in his holster. Don Fernando was still holding on tight to Dan's arm, but he bent down, picked up the book, stood up and handed it back to Dan, and whispered to him: "It's time to go now," and then dragged him out of the cell area. Oscar and María José Pavones followed, and Jorge Manuel brought up the rear.

They stepped back into the main lobby, where Oscar Pavones silently shook Jorge Manuel's hand, nodded towards don Fernando, and then he and María José Pavones quickly left the building.

Jorge Manuel signaled to the sergeant standing against the wall, "It appears the prisoner attempted to escape and you had to shoot him. Please arrange for the body to be shipped to the morgue... and have the cell cleaned and bleached."

"Yes sir," the sergeant replied, and went to his desk and got on the phone.

Don Fernando still had an iron grip on Dan's arm. He was whispering something to Jorge Manuel but Dan couldn't make it out. Jorge Manuel nodded in response to don Fernando, and then don Fernando, still holding Dan's arm, guided him out of the building, placed him in the front passenger seat of his car, then got in the driver's side, started the car, and began to drive back to Villa Rosario.

Dan head was pounding and he thought he was going to vomit. He had just witnessed a murder, a cold-blooded murder arranged by the police...the police he had helped.

"Pull the car over. I'm going to be sick," he said.

Don Fernando pulled the car over to the side of the

road quickly. Dan opened the door and vomited. He had not eaten breakfast, so all that come up was stomach juice mixed with the cup of coffee he had managed to brew and drink that morning. The acidic vomit burned his throat. He dry-heaved a bit more, took a deep breath, and sat back in the seat and closed the car door.

Finally now, at least, he could speak.

"You knew they were going to do that!" he said to don Fernando.

"Sí, señor."

"Don Fernando—that was murder!" Dan exclaimed.

"It is the old way, señor, true. We executed a murderer."

"But what if it wasn't him, don Fernando?" Dan asked.

"Jorge Manuel had a little chat with him this morning," don Fernando said, "and he was convinced... what is it you gringos say... beyond a reasonable doubt."

"That's not how it works!" Dan shouted. "You don't get to kill him just because you think he's guilty."

"It was not our decision, señor. In the old way, in the days of my grandfathers, the family of the victim got to make the decision. The Pavones elected to resurrect the old tradition—that is their right."

"Oh, fuck me," Dan said.

"I am not familiar with that expression, señor Dani, but I assume it means you do not agree with the old way. I understand that, and that is your right. But this is our country and our way. Sometimes the old ways are better."

"Don Fernando, what if the lab results don't point to that guy?"

"They will," don Fernando said, "I am pretty sure they will."

"Okay, but hypothetically speaking, what if they don't?" Dan asked.

"Hypothetically speaking? Well, I suppose, hypothetically speaking, those results would end up in the trash."

"Jesus," muttered Dan.

"Look señor Dani, what is the purpose of justice? It

is, first of all, finality. We have put an end to this monster. Secondly, it is to heal the community. Oscar and María José Pavones have been avenged—they can grieve for their son in peace now. Luis's bathhouse can re-open with assurances that the murderer is gone. Jorge Manuel will have the support of the Pavones family—and that is very important. The Pavones will buy uniforms and radios and even new patrol cars, so the city will be a safer place. And the public is spared the agony of a trial and publicity about the sordid things that go on in real life. No, señor Dani, it was better this way. It is the old way, but sometimes it is the better way." Don Fernando paused a bit, then added: "And if, hypothetically speaking, there is another murderer out there, and he strikes again, well, maybe it will be in another country, and if not, well, we'll deal with it then. We are no worse off."

"And what about the newspapers?" Dan asked.

"Well, as we told you before...." don Fernando started to say, but Dan interrupted him. "Oh yeah," Dan said. "They are owned by the Pavones."

"Right," said don Fernando. "There might be an article about a murder in an unnamed gay establishment, and about how the good police work of Jorge Manuel's team solved it, and unfortunately how the maniac murderer was shot trying to escape after he confessed, or there might be no mention of it at all... I don't know. I will leave those details up to the Pavones and Jorge Manuel. It is not our problem. Our work is done here."

"Jesus fucking Christ," was all Dan could say under his breath. He sat the rest of the ride in silence, just staring out the window.

Don Fernando turned the car's radio on and tuned in a station that played old Spanish ballads.

Chapter 16: LIFE

Two weeks passed by, and on this particular Thursday afternoon, Ricardo was sitting in the hot tub at the bathhouse in La Chorrera with his friend Miguel.

"I see business is booming here again," Miguel was saying, nodding towards the parade of beautiful men who strolled by the hot tub.

"Yes," Ricardo said, "well, I noticed that the owner has finally spent some money on advertising."

"Advertising and fixing the place up. Did you see he finally put a big flat screen in the video room, and new couches? Plus he's bought new porn to show on the TV. It looks really good." Miguel said.

"No, I hadn't wandered down that way yet," said Ricardo. "I'll have to check it out. I did notice new security cameras in the lobby."

"Ah yes," said Miguel, "that too. Well, better to be safe, I always say."

Just then, Luis walked up to the hot tub. Unlike Miguel and Ricardo, and the rest of the patrons in the bathhouse, Luis was dressed. He nodded at both men and said to Ricardo, "Disculpe, señor, are you don Ricardo?"

"I am," said Ricardo.

"They told me you were here," said Luis. "I am the owner here, and I just wanted to thank you. Our chief of police told me that you were very helpful to them in capturing that horrible man," and Luis extended his hand to Ricardo.

Ricardo shook the water off his hand and then shook Luis' hand. "It was just luck, señor, but I was glad to help. Anything that helps the bathhouse, helps me."

Luis laughed, "Sí, señor, well, that is true for me as well. But thank you again. You did us all a great service." And with that, Luis walked off.

"Well, that was nice," said Ricardo, "but it

would have been nicer if he had given me lifetime free admission."

Miguel chuckled and said, "But he is a businessman, don Ricardo. He knows you have no other place to go. He's not going to cut into his bottom line. But I think he was being sincere."

"Yeah... I agree," said Ricardo.

"The newspaper said that fellow tried to overpower a guard and escape and ended up getting shot dead for his efforts," said Miguel. "Evidently he was very violent."

"I heard about that," Ricardo said softly. Ricardo was quiet for a moment, and thought about how lucky he was to be alive.

Miguel seemed to read his mind. "It was a very brave thing you did, my friend," he said.

"It really was just blind luck," said Ricardo, "I really didn't do much."

"Luck favors the brave," said Miguel.

"Sometimes..." said Ricardo, "...and sometimes it just favors the foolish."

"Speaking of luck, my friend, I wonder how we will fare today?" said Miguel, and smiled.

"Well, maybe it's time we wandered off to the steam room and find out," replied Ricardo.

"I agree," said Miguel, and both men stood up.

*　　*　　*

As they walked down the hall towards the steam room, they did not notice Tacho mopping a side hallway. It was Tacho who had mentioned to Luis that Ricardo was at the bathhouse today, because Luis had shared with Tacho everything that Jorge Manuel had told him about the dangerous pursuit and capture of this maniac. And because Jorge Manuel had explained very clearly to Luis that they could not have captured the killer without Tacho's drawing, Luis had given Tacho a raise of half a balboa an hour, which meant that Tacho would be getting the equivalent of twenty extra dollars a week, which Tacho very much appreciated. Of course, Luis then decided to raise the admission fee by an extra balboa, which would cover Tacho's raise and help reimburse Luis for the new camera and new TV. It was Tacho who then suggested that Luis take out some advertisements in the local gay newspaper, and that had resulted in an upswing in attendance. Luis was pleased. Things were working well for everyone, he thought.

*   *   *

At the same moment that Ricardo and Miguel were reaching the steam room, Aaron was leaving his job a few minutes early to rush over to the bathhouse. His wife's meeting had been cancelled last week so it had been two weeks since he had been to the bathhouse, and he was feeling especially horny. Fortunately, his wife was going to her meeting today after work, so he would have that extra two hours of time. Maybe he would get lucky today, he thought, and find some strapping lad to ream him out, to bend him over and fuck him hard. The last time he had been at the bathhouse was two weeks ago, and he had been so disappointed during that visit—so he needed to get fucked today to make up for it. He even was wearing his special woman's panties today, for good luck.

*   *   *

Jared was not at the bathhouse today. He was in his doctor's office and they were discussing his viral load.

"You seem to be doing well, Jared," the doctor was saying, looking at Jared's most recent blood test. "It's important that you stay the course: continue to take your medicine, eat well, exercise, avoid alcohol, and of course, no illegal drugs. You continue to do all

128

these things, and you should be able to live a very normal life."

"Normal..." said Jared and looked away. He had been feeling particularly sad this past week, particularly lonely. Even the sex at the bathhouse had not seemed to stop the isolation he had been feeling recently. A normal life, he thought... what did that mean when you're VIH positive and cursed? What was normal anymore—to spend the rest of his life in a pitch black room waiting with his mouth open for the next cock? How is that normal? Jared wondered how long he would be able to endure this normality... weeks more, months more, years more?

His doctor looked at Jared. He knew his patients suffered emotionally, but he was only a medical doctor, not a psychologist. He only knew about blood counts and T-cells and viral transmissions. But still, he felt he had to say something.

"Have you tried any of those support groups? I gave you a list of them months ago," he asked Jared.

"No," Jared said, "I'm doing fine. I didn't see the need."

"You know, Jared," the doctor said, "the other day, I had a patient in here, a nice young man, very bright, very thoughtful... VIH positive just like you, and I thought of you... I thought that you two would make good friends. I can't tell you his name, you understand, because of patient confidentiality, but he told me that he belongs to a VIH positive gay dating site, that he was hoping to find a long-term partner... I wrote the website's name down here somewhere..." and the doctor began looking through his top desk drawer. "Ah yes, here it is... let me copy it down for you." The doctor took a pad of paper and wrote the name of the dating site on it, tore off the sheet of paper, and handed it to Jared. Jared looked at it. The doctor had written it on a prescription pad. Underneath the website name, the doctor had written "1 X week".

"I don't usually do this, but I am writing you a

prescription. When you leave here, I want you to go home and contact this place, and I want you to use this medicine once a week until you feel better, and thereafter, as needed."

Jared looked at the prescription again, and then at his doctor, and simply nodded his head and said, "Ok."

"Promise?" asked the doctor.

"I promise," said Jared.

And at the same moment that Miguel and Ricardo were stepping into the steam room, Dan was packing his suitcase. He had had a difficult two weeks, going over the events in his mind over and over, trying to reconcile them, but he couldn't. He hadn't necessarily been the most moral cop in L.A., but still... he believed in the system. He had had it ingrained in him just by growing up in the United States, and further hammered home at the police academy: the policeman's job was to catch the criminals, but it was the court's job to try them. He understood that the justice system was different in every country, but even though he had been an expat here for almost ten years, at his core, he was still a "norteamericano," a gringo, a yankee, and still held to that belief that only an impartial jury had the right to condemn an accused man.

He could not hold it against don Fernando for doing what he did. Don Fernando was born and raised here, and was correct when he had said that this was his country with its own ways of doing things. Besides, don Fernando was his friend, and their friendship went back many years. No, Dan could not blame don Fernando. In fact, Dan assumed that don Fernando's conscience was clean, and that so was Jorge Manuel's. But Dan's wasn't, and he had not had a good night's sleep since Esteban had been murdered.

Dan continued to fold shirts and place them in his suitcase. He had decided he needed to take a small vacation—a vacation back to the states. He would keep his apartment here, because he knew he would come back, but for now, he needed to go home for a bit.... "*home*"...he grimaced when he realized he was thinking of the states that way. He had left there angry and bitter almost ten years ago after he had been falsely accused of tipping off some gang members about a police raid... but that was water under the bridge now. Ten years is a long time, and while time does not ever heal any wound, it can cover them up with enough layers of other experiences that the bleeding stops. But he wouldn't go back to L.A. No point in tearing open the scars that covered those wounds. He had bought an airplane ticket to Las Vegas, Nevada. Las Vegas was the perfect place to get a grip on life, or to disappear for awhile, or both. He still had a few friends there he could crash with. He had already spoken to them on the phone. He could establish temporary residency by using their address, and convert his expired California driver's license to a Nevada driver's license. Maybe he would buy a used car and just travel around the old West. Maybe he would get a job as a security guard at a casino. Maybe he would just gamble and drink. He just wanted to go somewhere where the rules made sense, somewhere where he could just feel normal again, somewhere where he could just forget, and just zone out for three or four months... then maybe he'd be somehow healed, somehow restored... and then he could come back here and feel okay again. Don Fernando was still his best friend, and Ricardo was a good friend. Maybe when he came back he could learn to accept "the old ways" here, but not now. He wasn't ready for that yet. For now, he needed to get away, go home for a bit and heal..."*home*"...that damn word again.

He had gone over to Jenny's brothel the night before, to have sex with Magali one more time and to tell her that he would be gone for a while. She took the news of his leaving as he had expected—without any emotion. But she did seem to fuck him especially well after he told her... maybe she still did have some feelings for him... or maybe she was just making sure he'd remember to ask for her when he came back. Either way, it had been good—she always seemed to reach him in such a special way. Oddly enough, the fact that the sex had been so good made him even more committed to leave. It seemed to give him a taste of how much better he needed to feel... how much better he could feel when he got back home in the states... "home"...there was that word again. Maybe home is simply where you go when you need some place to heal, he thought.

*　　*　　*

And that's how life is, my friends: it goes on, with you or without you... but it goes on. Life in La Chorrera will go on without Esteban, and no one will miss him. No one will know how he lived, and no one, except those few who were there, will know how he died. And only a handful will remember what he even looked like, and even that memory will fade as time moves on, although the image of the side of his head being blown off will haunt Dan for many years.

And life in La Chorrera will go on without Ernesto too, although the memory of him will persist vividly with his family for the rest of their lives. His parents buried him in a private ceremony. The casket was the finest that money could buy. Ernesto always had the finest that money could buy, because deep in their hearts, his parents always knew that his life would be short, and full of suffering... blind, deaf, and dumb.

And that's how life is too, my friends: it is short, full of suffering, and blind, deaf, and dumb. That's how it was for Ernesto, and that's how it is for Ricardo, Miguel, Dan, and for you and for me. We are all feeling our way through the dark, either by mere touch, or by pretending to be someone we're not, or by blind luck. And yet, there are those moments

132

sometimes... when we are feeling our way blindly... whether it's the dark steamy corridors or simply the darkest moments of our lives... when our fingers touch someone else's flesh in the darkness, and for that brief moment, that touch fills us with hope... hope for someone or something that will transport us out of suffering and into the light, if only to heal for a little while. Maybe it's a person we long for... or maybe it's a place... or maybe it's an idea... but it's always someone or something that feels like home to us, that draws us towards him or her or it... but it's a home we've never really known... and so we keep searching for it. Dan will fly to Vegas, and Ricardo and Miguel will continue to cruise the dark hallways, and Aaron will dream of the perfect fuck, and Jared will grieve for love, and Oscar and María José Pavones will grieve for the son who was never quite whole. For none of us are really whole. We're all blind and deaf and dumb. And all life is, my friends, is a journey to a home we never reach.

-FIN-

ABOUT THE AUTHOR

Over the past 30 years, Robert Rahula has published dozens books of prose and poetry in Spain and in the United States. While he remains relatively undiscovered in the United States, he is revered in Spain as the founder of the "portilla" style of popular Spanish poetry: non-metered fluid verse that deals with love, loss, bisexuality, separateness, and growing older.

Robert was born in Spain to an American father and Spanish mother, but grew up in Virginia on the farm of his paternal grandparents. He returned to Menorca, Spain, in the 1960s to pursue his writing career. These days he travels in Europe, Central and South America for several months a year, giving readings and lectures, and spends the rest of his time writing, dividing his time between Spain and the United States.

All of Robert's English books are available through Amazon Kindle, including his groundbreaking erotic novel Messieurs; his second English novel Panamaniac; his erotic murder mystery Island of Misfits; his surreal novel Day Another Paradise In; his acclaimed supernatural novel One Last Fling; his "sexistential" novel Conversations in a Belgian Bar; as well as his three "Dan Landes Mystery" novels: Bathhouse Stories, All the Yage in Reno, and Exigent Circumstances. A new volume of short stories, Horror Stories for Children, is available in both ebook and print versions.

Seven volumes of Robert's English poetry are also available on Amazon: Trigger Points; Inside the Locked Heart; Camino; Migration; I Sing the Body Politic; Wonderland; From Whose Bourn; as well as an anthology of his English poems and short stories, Half-Life; a collection of his most famous Spanish poems, Poemas Españoles; and his anthology of expatriate poetry, Expat Poems. Other poems, along with his blog on writing and his tour itinerary, appear on his Facebook page and on his website robertrahula.com.